Of Time and Place

Of Time and Place

A Lineage Series Novel

Michael Paul Hurd

Lineage Independent Publishing
Marriottsville, MD

This is a work of fiction. The characters, relationships, dialogue, and incidents other than established historical facts are drawn from the author's imagination and should not be construed as portrayals of real events.

ISBN (paperback): 9781958418178
First Printed in the United States

Publisher: Lineage Independent Publishing, Marriottsville, MD

Maryland Sales and Use Tax Entity: Lineage Independent Publishing, Marriottsville, MD 21104

Contact: hurdmp@lineage-indypub.com

Website: https://lineage-indypub.com

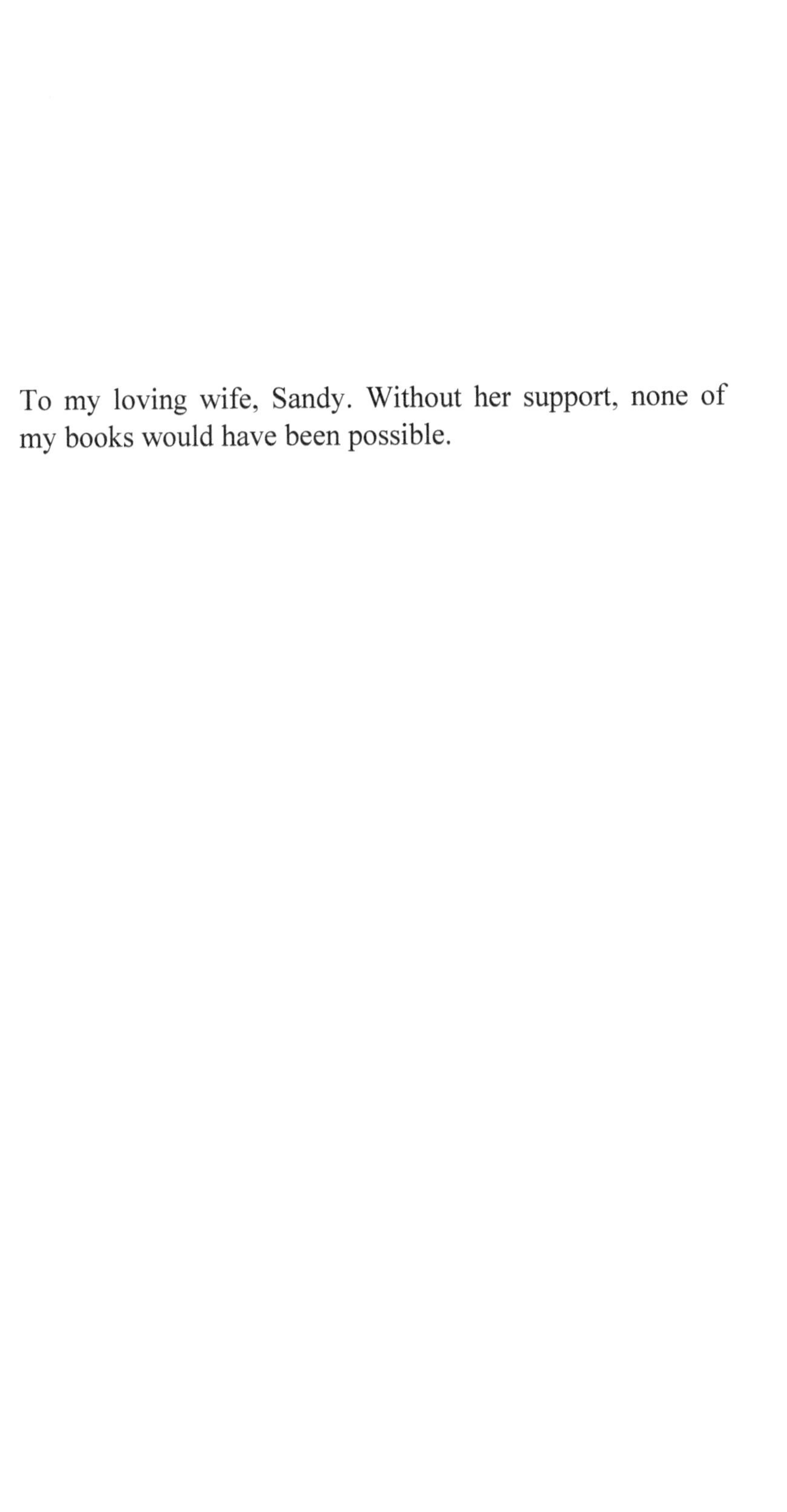

To my loving wife, Sandy. Without her support, none of my books would have been possible.

Contents

Crossing the Bar

Sunset and evening star,
And one clear call for me!
And may there be no moaning of the bar,
When I put out to sea,

But such a tide as moving seems asleep,
Too full for sound and foam,
When that which drew from out the boundless deep
Turns again home.

Twilight and evening bell,
And after that the dark!
And may there be no sadness of farewell,
When I embark;

For tho' from out our bourne of Time and Place
The flood may bear me far,
I hope to see my Pilot face to face
When I have crost the bar.

Alfred, Lord Tennyson

As a child and teenager, if I wasn't playing sports, I was reading. My favorite genre' was always science fiction. It allowed total escape into 'what could be' versus 'what has been.' Time travel, teleportation, and intergalactic travel all fascinated me. That is, until I was appointed to the United States Naval Academy.

My four years at the Academy taught me to question everything, to analyze, to make judgments only on the basis of facts at hand. Still, I kept one foot in my fantasy world but not for escapism; instead, it was a way of showing me what might be theoretically possible.

Take Einstein's Theory of Relativity, for example: an observer traveling near the speed of light, approximately 186,000 miles per second, will experience 'time' much more slowly than an observer at rest on a singular point in our galactic world. Though it might be possible to slow the advance of current time in relation to a datum point, Einstein did not suggest that reversing time, or even going backward on a timeline, was even conceivable.

Moving out into the real world of military operations after graduation and commissioning, I became a Special Warfare Officer. A trained killer. A stealthy reconnaissance operator. A survival expert. It was in that world where I spent the totality of my naval career and eventually met the love of my life, Bethany Kimmel, a distant relative of Admiral Husband E. Kimmel – the Commander in Chief of the United States Navy's Pacific Fleet on December 7, 1941.

My own family tree was not as illustrious. I came from humble roots, immigrants to the American Colonies in the 1600s. Most settled in what is now Connecticut. I am, however, fortunate that the branches of my family tree are solid, traceable back to at least the time of Charles II in England.

There were some members of my family tree who were Royalists or sided with them in the English Civil Wars. Family legends suggest that they may have been involved with Charles II's escape from England after the Battle of Worcester in 1651.

There was plenty of "down time" during my military career, time that allowed me to think and to speculate on my ancestors. When I wasn't working out to maintain the level of fitness required for combat readiness, I was role playing their lives in my mind. How did they come to the New World? Did they miss those left behind? Did they ever return to England or receive letters from loved ones?

Little did I know that I was going to be given a chance to see their stories first-hand…

Chapter One: A State of Confusion
Somewhere in the Atlantic Ocean

As I gradually became aware of my surroundings, the smell of unwashed bodies, human waste, and vomit assaulted my nostrils, eliciting a reflexive gag. In the semi-darkness, my eyes were having trouble focusing, perhaps because of the salt crystals that were washing into my eyes. Where was I? Was this God's idea of a prank to be endured on my way to hell?

Not yet fully coherent and still somewhat disoriented, my last conscious memory was that of being adrift in a small rescue rowboat on the open ocean. Scanning the horizon, I could see nothing but mile upon mile of calm blue water in any direction. I expected to see my inherited yacht, a 75-foot Maritimo christened the *Great Escape* by my father, somewhere nearby, but there was not even the slightest scrap of flotsam or jetsam – nor any bodies – anywhere to be seen. Had I been abandoned, or was there a terrible accident that left me as the sole survivor?

*　*　*　*　*

The 16-foot fiberglass and foam dinghy, named *Great Escape II,* was intended to be a vessel of last resort. It was equipped with a very small outboard motor and five gallons of fuel, four oars, a supply of fresh water and shelf-stable surplus rations from the military, "Meals, Ready to Eat" or MREs in military parlance. There were also six personal flotation devices (PFDs), handlines for fishing, sunblock, docking lines, and a tarp that could be used as either a sail or shade from the unrelenting sun. As I was becalmed and adrift in an underlying current, I used the docking lines to lash the tarp in place over the aft third of the boat to shade me from the blistering sunshine.

In a waterproof container under the center bench, there was a handheld VHF radio. I checked the batteries, and they were fully charged. Keying the "transmit" button, I called a "Mayday," repeating the emergency call and the name of my dinghy at thirty second intervals for half an hour. Perhaps I had drifted out of the shipping lanes and out of radio range of any vessels. Handhelds had an effective range of only three to eight nautical miles, so any large vessels within radio range should also have been within visual range. Instead, the sea was completely empty to the horizon in all directions.

Somehow, the rowboat had been set free from the davits on the stern of the *Great Escape.* It would have taken human intervention to release the safety interlocks. I had no memory of ever having released the little boat from those davits – but somehow, it happened and here I am.

I developed a ration plan for the fuel, water and MREs and set about trying to catch a fish for additional sustenance. It didn't take long before I had landed a small mahi-mahi and dispatched it with a swift stroke of the stainless-steel survival knife. The razor-sharp knife would be my salvation for the days to come; each fish I caught was quickly filleted and eaten raw and I kept the entrails to use as bait. The last thing I wanted was to be without either bait or artificial lures, as they were essential to my nutrition and survival.

I also used the knife to carefully scrape a mark on the starboard side gunwale for each sunset I observed. Doing so would help my eventual rescuers (assuming I was still alive, that is!) confirm how long I had been adrift. The days turned into more than two weeks and the boredom was broken only by the monotony of it all.

Having enough water was always a challenge, so I devised a system to use the tarp to catch the water whenever it rained. It didn't taste the best after running down a dirty tarp and into an empty water ration bottle –

but it kept me hydrated. Water, my military survival school had taught me, was always more important than food.

Five gallons of fuel was not nearly enough to propel me any considerable distance, so I chose to push west for no more than an estimated 20 minutes a day. It would not keep me from drifting further from shore, but it could keep me drifting within the northeasterly offshore currents. The fuel ran out after my tenth day adrift, so I jettisoned the motor and the fuel tank. Doing so improved *Great Escape II*'s stability and allowed me to move more freely around the small boat without over-weighting the stern area.

By my own counting, I had been adrift for about three weeks when my awareness of the present changed. I was awakened in the middle of the night with the dinghy being tossed about like a cork in a swimming pool full of children playing "Marco Polo." Rather than take any further risks, I donned a PFD from the small compartment under the seat and settled down into the keel as best I could, hoping that my little boat would not capsize. The sea calmed just before dawn and I settled into a fitful slumber that lasted through almost all of the next day; I woke only to relieve myself, hydrate, take a few bites of raw fish.

The day-long slumber was the first time I had not made an effort to issue a mid-day "Mayday" call on the radio since being separated from the *Great Escape*. When I woke around sunset. I spent about 30 minutes transmitting the call with no response. "I must be out of radio range and out of the shipping lanes," I said aloud to myself before switching off the radio once again to conserve its battery. The integrated solar charger provided only a "trickle charge" that would not keep pace with continual use.

The fact that I was catching mahi-mahi gave me some idea as to my whereabouts. I knew that the species was a warm water loving fish and that the Atlantic from the East Coast of the United States out to the Gulf Stream tended to be colder water. The Gulf Stream, however, was significantly warmer and provided an ideal habitat for mahi-mahi. I quickly deduced that I was drifting northeast and somewhere off the coast of the Delmarva Peninsula.

The inky blackness of night falls quickly on the open sea and I was left alone with my thoughts. As the darkness deepened, so did my mood. Never having been a praying man, I was now praying for my very life. Seemingly in answer to those prayers, a blinding flash of lightning lit the night sky and the dark sea around me. In that brief instant, I saw the spectral shadow of what appeared to be a large

17th Century sailing ship just before the percussion from the thunderclap knocked me into senseless oblivion. I had no recollection of the next several hours – or were they days? Weeks? Even longer?

*　　*　　*　　*　　*

As I awoke, I suddenly realized that I was onboard the sailing ship I had seen silhouetted by the lightning bolt. My brain, though, could not reconcile the primitive conditions on the ship, nor the fact that my caretaker was a young black woman, naked from the waist up. Carefully offering me a sip of fetid water from a nearby bucket, she spoke in a language that I neither recognized nor understood. I had learned both Arabic and Pashto in the Navy – and what she was saying did not seem to have any words in common with either of those tongues. Her tone, though, was soothing and I quickly determined that she meant me no harm. She tenderly cleaned my sun-blistered back and upper body, considerably reducing my discomfort.

Pointing unashamedly between her breasts, the woman established that her name was *"Fatou."* She was not the least bit self-conscious about her exposed breasts as she spoke. I had heard of African cultures where women did not cover themselves, even in the 21st Century, and wondered if she had come from one of those areas.

The unanswered question was "Where am I?" or more importantly *"When* am I?" as it seemed that I was no longer in the 21st Century. I tried to ask those questions, but Fatou could only smile and shake her head. She did not appear to understand a word I was saying.

My confusion must have come across as delirium from sun exposure. My head and body twitched as I rapidly scanned the environment for threats, something that my military training had taught me to do. Though I looked like a long-tailed cat in a room full of rocking chairs, the quick visual scans of my immediate surroundings provided more information than prolonged fixation on a single object. I could not determine any immediate threats to my safety, but I was still confused by the conditions under which Fatou was caring for me.

As my awareness of the surroundings increased, I looked up and saw the shadows and rigging for a two-masted sailing ship. Missing from my observations was any stainless steel hardware – which would have been normal on any sailing vessel from *my* time – and the associated "clang, clank, clang" of that rigging against an aluminum mast. Everything I saw was made of wood or forged from iron and the ropes appeared to have been rough hand-braided hemp rather than smooth-running nylon.

After what seemed like an eternity, a white man in clothing that appeared to be a merchant officer's uniform strode down to the main deck from the elevated helm at the aft of the ship. I noticed immediately that he had a coiled leather whip stuffed inside his waist sash. I was puzzled.

"Good day, sir!" the officer boomed. "We rescued you from the jaws of Hell itself. We were nigh certain that you were going to leave us, save for Fatou's ministrations. I am Joshua Hailey, First Officer of the 'Desire'."

As Hailey extended his hand in greeting, he asked, "What name do they call you, sir? I must have it added to the Captain's Log and to our manifest."

"My name is Jonathan Harris," I replied. "I come from…"

Thinking that my knowledge of geography and placenames might not match with the reality on board the *Desire,* I paused to choose my next words carefully.

"I am from Jamestown and was set adrift some miles off the mouth of the Chesapeake Bay. I believe my ship sank beneath me in a storm." As I could not prove anything to the contrary, this would be my story going forward. "I might be the sole survivor."

"Aye, sir. Your story makes perfect sense, but your small dinghy is made of a strange material," Hailey observed, "and your clothing, or what's left of it, is like nothing we have ever seen before on the high seas."

Again, I was caught between my world and his. In my world, fiberglass was the normal material for hull construction for vessels small and large. In his world, that material and additional foam flotation would not be invented for almost another three centuries. Wood, or more specifically oak, was the shipwright's material of choice for 17th Century ships of sail. I had studied the construction of such sailing ships during my time at the United States Naval Academy in Annapolis.

"It is, Mr. Hailey, but I fear that it will not last and I recommend you destroy it forthwith." That period in history was fraught with superstitions, so I added, "There may be demons in her hull, and I am afraid they will inhabit your fine ship in due time." I knew instantly that I was destroying the one thing that might connect me with my own timeline, but it was better to have the dinghy destroyed than it was to be tossed overboard as a result of the prevailing superstitions of the day.

Hailey thought for a moment, then summoned the ship's carpenter and four able seamen to his side. "Men, take Mr. Harris's dinghy and hole it below the waterline. It is possessed and needs to be on its way to the devil in the deep blue sea."

In unison, the men responded "Aye, Sir!"

Using a brace and bit, the seamen bored several holes into the hull of my dingy and unceremoniously lowered it over the side. It quickly filled with water – as expected – but did not sink. Hailey was perplexed and called for the Captain.

What I hadn't accounted for was the flotation chambers and foam hidden in the seats and gunwales of the *Great Escape II*. Its manufacturer's sales literature insisted that such a craft would be unsinkable, even when totally swamped.

Hailey wanted to fire the small deck guns at my now unsalvageable dinghy to hasten its sinking. However, it was the standing policy on board the *Desire* that the deck guns were not to be fired without Captain's orders and this time was no different. One of the seamen was dispatched to summon the Captain to the deck.

The Captain, a strapping man nearly a head taller than the rest of the crew, appeared from his cabin below the helm. "Mister Hailey! Report!"

"Aye, Sir. We have rescued a man from the sea, a Mister Jonathan Harris, from Jamestown in the Virginia Colony."

The Captain turned to me and touched the brim of his hat in recognition of my presence. "Welcome, Mister Harris, to the *Desire*. I am Captain John Palmer at your service."

Before I could respond, Palmer turned back to Hailey and barked, "Continue, please, Mister Hailey." Palmer was all business and seemed to run a very tightly disciplined ship.

"Aye, Sir. Mister Harris believes his small dinghy may be possessed by demons and I have ordered it to be sent to the depths. The ship's carpenter and his men bored holes in its hull, but it does not sink. I recommend, Sir, that we fire the deck guns and blast it to splinters."

"A good choice, Mister Hailey. It will give the men a chance to practice their marksmanship... Gunner! Make the deck guns ready for three salvos. All hands on watch, prepare your weapons for firing five rounds each," Captain Palmer ordered.

The next several minutes were alive with the sounds and smells of musket and cannon fire, mixed with the good-natured cajoling of the crew. Those that missed their shots were teased mercilessly by those whose shots found their mark. I estimated that it took less than fifteen minutes for the dingy to be completely shredded by the gunfire and sent to the bottom of the ocean. *There goes my connection to the 21st Century..."* I thought sadly.

Palmer turned to me again after the smoke had cleared. "Mister Harris, as a guest on board the *Desire*, I request that you dine with me this evening in my quarters… after a good wash and a shave, that is. I run a tight ship and cleanliness is next to godliness, I always say!:

"Yes, Captain. I shall be honored," I replied.

What would we talk about over dinner? Would it be just me and Captain Palmer on our own? Would I find out anything about our whereabouts or cargo? I thought about ways of eliciting information from Captain Palmer that would not pique his suspicions. I also had to prepare for the inevitable interrogation about my background and origins.

What was a believable backstory beyond what I had already told Hailey?

Hailey understood that it was his duty to ensure that I was properly bathed and attired for dinner. My clothing, or more what was left of my clothing, hung immodestly from my gaunt frame like rags. It would be thrown overboard once I was issued something more suitable.

Taken to a private area out of sight of the prying eyes of the crew, Hailey indicated I should undress. As if out of nowhere, Fatou appeared with a bucket of water and scented soap. It was clear that she intended to wash me from head to toe.

"Think nothing of it, Mister Harris. Fatou is at our service and takes good care of the officers, if you catch my meaning," Hailey said with a twinkle in his eye.

Fatou bathed me from head to toe, pausing to observe the surgical scars on my lower back and buttocks, then shaved my beard with one of the sharpest straight razors I had ever experienced. She could have just as easily opened my neck and bled me to death right there on the deck. Once she had completed the shave, she combed and coiffed my hair; it certainly was unruly after who-knows-how-long I was adrift in my dinghy.

Her tenderness was like nothing I had experienced before, not even while I was convalescing at the Walter Reed National Military Medical Center after being wounded in combat in a country I couldn't talk about. The nurses and orderlies there were all business. Though they were a caring bunch overall, they were still military and had to avoid emotional attachment to their charges, some of whom had experienced the most horrific injuries. Fortunately, I was not deprived of any of my limbs, organs, or senses – but I was now equipped with an artificial hip joint and a permanent limp favoring my right side. The recovery – and learning to walk again – had taken several months.

*   *   *   *   *

I entered the Captain's Quarters just as the sun was sinking below the horizon off our port bow. That told me we were on a westerly base course. Generally spartan and functional, the Captain's accommodations were still more lavish than those for the rest of the crew. The officers were bunked two to a cabin, while the men slept in hammocks in forward areas on the second deck. Below them were the cargo holds.

Captain Palmer was just finishing his daily log entry, which he read aloud to me, "27th of August, in the Year of Our Lord 1654: added one castaway to the ship's complement, a Mister Jonathan Harris, from Jamestown in the Virginia Colony. Mister Harris was rescued from his dinghy at an approximate position of 34 degrees north, 74 degrees and 30 minutes west. This position is roughly halfway between His Majesty's Colony on Bermuda and the Carolina coast."

I could hardly hide my incredulity when Palmer read the date. It was the middle of the 17th Century! I had somehow traveled back in time over 350 years. I stared blankly into space, hypnotized by the reality, until I was suddenly brough back by the sound of the Captain's voice.

"Mister Harris, I trust that boiled beef, potatoes, and rum will suit your fancy?" Captain Palmer inquired.

"Of course, Sir. I have been living on raw fish for quite some time," I replied. I felt that keeping my answers terse and to the point was appropriate until I had a better sense of what lay in store for me on the *Desire*.

"Mister Hailey tells me that you have no idea how you came to be with us, nor what caused the demise of your ship…"

For the next several hours, I gleaned as much information as I could from Captain Palmer. At the same time, I was careful not to divulge any of my own details that could be proven to be inaccurate in 1654. In the end, I knew as much as there was to know about the *Desire*, its crew, and its disgusting cargo of human slaves. For his part, Captain Palmer also tried to get as much information as he could out of me, but I remained as taciturn as I could under the circumstances, not volunteering any information unless directly asked. I had to maintain my credibility, and in order to do that, I had to keep my story simple.

Chapter Two: Aboard the *Great Escape*
June 2015

"Mayday, Mayday, Mayday…this is the motor vessel *Great Escape* on Channel 1-6. Mayday, Mayday, Mayday. Any vessel or aircraft within range please acknowledge. Over." Bethany Harris repeated the "Mayday" call several times, with about a thirty second interval between each repeat.

"*Great Escape*, this is the United States Coast Guard Cutter *Hamilton*. State the nature of your emergency. Over."

"*Hamilton*, this is *Great Escape*. We seem to have a person overboard and missing at sea. Over."

"*Great Escape*, switch and answer, Channel 2-2 Alfa."

"Roger, *Hamilton*. Channel 2-2 Alfa."

It took only a few seconds for Bethany to switch the radio channel, as Jonathan had pre-programmed the Coast Guard's "working" channel into the radio's presets. Pressing one button, labeled "ALT" on the radio's controls, tuned the radio to the new frequency and broadcast its transponder information to the Coast Guard.

"*Great Escape*, this is *Hamilton* on Channel 2-2 Alfa. Say your position. Over."

"Our current position is 35 decimal 554158 North, 74 decimal 062418 West. Over." Bethany read the coordinates from the yacht's Automated Identification System, or AIS for short.

"*Great Escape*, this is *Hamilton*. We confirm your position from AIS. When was the missing person last seen on board your vessel? Over."

"*Hamilton*, the missing person is a 50-year-old male last seen on board around 0300 hours UTC this morning." Bethany Harris was well-versed in proper radio procedures; she had been a naval communications officer for several years before meeting Jonathan. It was their normal procedure to keep the *Great Escape* on Universal Time Coordinated, or UTC, when they were on the open ocean. It was easier than worrying about what time zone they might be in. She continued, "Our position log at that time was 38 decimal 383300 North, 72 decimal 87166 West."

"Roger, *Great Escape*. If possible, hold current position as search datum. We are approximately 25 nautical miles due west of you. Launching Search and Rescue helicopter to your AIS position. *Hamilton*'s ETA approximately 90 minutes. Over."

The *Great Escape* was equipped with the latest in civilian maritime technology; this included a GPS-calibrated autopilot which was integrated with the vessel's radar. The mere mortal on the bridge was there more as a failsafe and to monitor the mechanical condition of the engines and electrical systems.

It had been more than eight hours since Jonathan Harris had been seen aboard his yacht. Bethany suddenly realized that she might have been the last person to see her husband alive. She was also keenly aware that she could have dozed off at the helm not long after replacing her husband at the auxiliary helm on the flybridge.

Their traveling companions, Byron and Virginia Lattimore, had retired early and were preoccupied with what was happening in their stateroom. Over dinner, the other couple had been inappropriately demonstrative with their physical affections and intentions. Bethany knew exactly what had gone on in their stateroom during the night and she was more than a little bit jealous that the other couple was more interested in marital relations than sharing the work that went into safely operating a large vessel like the *Great Escape*.

Lost in her own thoughts for a few moments and thinking the worst, Bethany was startled when the Coast Guard helicopter overflew the yacht. The VHF radio crackled to life.

"*Great Escape*, this is Coast Guard Helicopter 6002, overhead your position on Channel 2-2 Alfa. Request permission to lower our search coordinator and equipment to your aft deck."

"Roger, Coast Guard. Permission granted," Bethany replied. She knew from her Navy days that she had to stay clear of the winch line that was lowering the search coordinator and his equipment. One wrong touch and the static electric discharge could be strong enough to knock her overboard. There was already one person missing; she had no intention of being the second.

Alighting on the aft deck, the search coordinator quickly detached himself from his safety harness and motioned for Bethany that it was clear for her to approach. As she did so, the Lattimores emerged from their cabin, not quite grasping what was happening. Seeing the Coast Guard officer on deck was unnerving.

"Ma'am, I am Commander Adrian Maxwell. I will be coordinating the search for your missing husband. What was your course and speed at the presumed time of his disappearance?"

For the next several minutes, Commander Maxwell grilled Bethany Harris and the Lattimores for additional information on Jonathan and his disappearance. Maxwell also checked the yacht from stem to stern, including the staterooms, for clues. The Lattimores were of little help: they had spent the night in their stateroom engaged in "adult recreation," as they told Maxwell with sheepish grins. *"They didn't have to confirm what I already knew,"* Bethany thought to herself, surprised at the biting tone of her own thoughts.

Reaching the stern davits where the dinghy had once been secured, Maxwell noticed something that even the detail-minded Bethany Harris might have overlooked.

"Mrs. Harris, it seems that the release of the dinghy from the davits was intentional," Maxwell commented. "The lines were cut, I think, with a dull knife."

"I should have seen that. I am a retired naval officer with extensive sea service," she replied. "Though I was a communications officer, I was command rated and know a thing or two about lines."

"It's understandable that you overlooked it, given your husband's disappearance," Maxwell replied.

Bethany bristled at the implications of this youngster's flippant tone. "Commander, my husband is a retired naval officer as well, a Captain… his service… well… we can't exactly talk about it, but he is a survival expert and was wounded multiple times. It certainly wasn't *his* knife that cut the dinghy's mooring lines – he always kept it razor-sharp."

"Thank you, ma'am," Maxwell acknowledged. He was somewhat taken aback by Bethany's defensive reply.

At that moment, Maxwell's handheld VHF radio crackled with a call from the Search and Rescue helicopter. "Search Coordinator, this is 6002. No joy. Search radius 20 miles from your position. Over."

"002, Roger." The tone of Maxwell's reply was all business and devoid of any emotion. Over his career of nearly two decades, this was not his first unsuccessful search, nor would it be his last. He had learned long ago to remain entirely professional in his dealings with survivors.

"Mrs. Harris, we are dispatching a Hercules from Elizabeth City. It will have considerably more range than our helicopter. It will have to return to the *Hamilton* to refuel in about two hours. Until then, it will continue expanding the search radius out from this position. As close as you are to the Gulf Stream, it is possible that your husband's dinghy got caught in the strong current and could be a considerable distance north of here. We will also put out a NOTAM… Notice to All Mariners… to be on the lookout for the dinghy and, hopefully, your husband."

Twelve hours later, the search was still unsuccessful and called off for darkness. The *Hamilton* remained nearby on a slow and parallel course. Its crew scanned the water until dawn with both night vision goggles and infrared sensors. Bethany Harris began to prepare herself for the likelihood that Jonathan would be declared missing and presumed dead.

Not totally accepting the reality of Jonathan's evanescence, Bethany spent the next several hours being comforted by the Lattimores. She could have more easily dealt with Jonathan being a casualty of war, dying in the service of his country. Instead, she now had to deal with a suspicious disappearance and the possibility that Jonathan had suffered a mental health crisis of some kind. The stress of the past fifteen hours, combined with an increasing groundswell, caused Bethany Harris to become violently seasick for the first time in her life.

Once the waves of nausea passed (aided by the application of a scopolamine patch behind her left ear), Bethany took charge of the *Great Escape* and set a course for the mouth of the Chesapeake Bay. Once inside the Chesapeake Bay Bridge-Tunnel, she would head for the Navy's Recreation Facility and its marina at Norfolk Naval Station. After an overnight stay, refueling, and reprovisioning, it was about a 12-hour cruise north to Annapolis.

Chapter Three: Shipboard Routines
Aboard the *Desire*, 1654

After dinner with Captain Palmer and several rations of potent rum, I was shown to my quarters by the Deck Officer of the watch. There were two berths in the cabin, the lower of which was occupied by a sleeping form that did not stir when I entered. I climbed into the upper berth and quickly fell into a deep sleep.

When I awoke, the lower bunk was empty, and it appeared to be daylight. After the Captain's dinner, I had no concept of time or place; I could have been asleep for an entire week – or was I just waking up from a bad dream? The creaking of the ship's timbers and the human groans coming from someplace deep inside the vessel told me that I was indeed in the Year of Our Lord 1654 as I had been told by Captain Palmer after our introduction.

I suddenly realized that I needed to relieve myself and made my way to the head. That pretty much confirmed I wasn't locked in a nightmare. As I traversed forward from the stern, I was puzzled. The day before, I had only seen Fatou, the able seamen, and First Officer Hailey. Now there were approximately 100 nearly naked black men shackled together at the ankles, walking in a counterclockwise circle around the main deck. I quickly surmised it was one of their exercise periods. They must have been captured in Africa with the intention for them to be enslaved.

When I returned from the head, two of the black men were carrying what appeared to be a shrouded body to the port side. It was laid on a plank and unceremoniously levered over the railing. Not a word or prayer was spoken.

The deck was then cleared and a group of about 50 women, all naked from the waist up, were brought up to the main deck for their exercise period. The comments from the white men were anything but polite; it was probably fortunate that the women did not understand what was being said about them.

The final group, consisting of about 50 men, came up to the main deck. They seemed to be the most frail of the lot, perhaps because they had been relegated to the lowest level of the hold and the most cramped conditions. I feared for their lives and wondered if they would see land again in their lifetime.

I noticed that in all three of the groups, there were more than a couple of bodies that bore the welts of recent beatings. That seemed to explain the coiled whip stuffed in

First Officer Hailey's belt. I hadn't yet witnessed any such punishment, but it was only a matter of time before I likely would see a flogging first-hand.

"Mister Hailey, how many more days do we expect to be at sea?" I asked when I finally located the First Officer.

"Mister Harris, we are about a week out from New Haven and its slave market," he responded. "We could put in at a nearer port – but Captain Palmer has a contract to deliver this human cargo... *these slaves...* to the New Haven market, in the Connecticut Colony.

"New Haven?" I thought to myself. I knew there had been slaves in the northern colonies before the Civil War – but was not aware that there was a slave market in New Haven. I couldn't let my knowledge of the future, nor my ignorance of the 17th Century, affect my actions any more than necessary. It was up to me to assimilate into the *Desire*'s daily routines.

*　*　*　*　*

In all my studies of history at the Naval Academy in the 20th Century, we never discussed slavery in the northern states, just the ones south of the Mason-Dixon line that seceded from the Union and formed the Confederate States of America. I knew that the northern colonies had slaves, but the facts of slavery in the north were conveniently brushed aside; even notables like Philip Schuyler in New York had owned slaves. Yet here I was, on board a slave ship bound for New Haven in the Connecticut Colony. My curiosity was piqued, and I wanted to learn more.

Bethany and I had visited Connecticut many times during our years together, mostly after our retirements from the Navy. The coast was rich with sheltered places to anchor the *Great Escape* and venture ashore in our little dinghy that was now at the bottom of the ocean. Now I would be given a chance to see what it looked like over 350 years earlier – and there was a good chance I could even meet one of my own ancestors.

I knew the Harris family had roots in Connecticut and Massachusetts. Several generations of my ancestors had lived there before, during and after the Revolutionary War. It was a family legend that a Lieutenant Thomas Harris fought alongside Aaron Burr at Monmouth and Alexander Hamilton at Yorktown. Family records also told of Thomas Harris's descendants migrating west following American independence, eventually settling in what was then known as the Northwest Territory.

The possibility of meeting up with an ancestor intrigued me. With a "generation" generally established as 20 years, I would be interacting with someone at least seventeen or eighteen generations earlier in the family tree, a separation so great that I would have very little DNA in common with them. Just considering the possibilities mentally exhausted me.

*   *   *   *   *

I asked First Officer Hailey to include me in the watch schedule as a forward lookout. There, I could make myself useful to the *Desire* while not letting my knowledge of seamanship be known. At Annapolis, we were all taught celestial navigation using a sextant – but they were not yet invented in 1654. Sailors of that period might have used a quadrant for navigation, but its application was rudimentary compared to the relative precision of the sextant.

Crew life aboard a sailing vessel in the 17th Century was anything but glamorous. It was arduous and dangerous. Watches rotated as eight hours on duty, then eight hours off. Seafarers quickly learned to sleep whenever and wherever they could – and I was no different. Having served an entire career as a Special Warfare officer in the United States Navy of the 20th and 21st Centuries, I had mastered the concept of sleeping on command. Though I had been retired for several years, the capability had quickly returned to me. It made my life aboard the *Desire* tolerable.

The next week was a blur of standing watch, sleeping, and eating. I could tell we were getting close to our destination when I could smell the smoke from the cooking fires of settlements beyond the horizon to the west. The aromas were definitely more appealing than the slop our ship's cook called "food." I couldn't wait to get ashore to have a proper meal, even one cooked in the 17th Century's unhygienic conditions.

Before we headed for port, we had more dead bodies to dispose of. This time, there were six: four men and two women. They were cast over the side just as unceremoniously as the first group I had observed several days earlier. The conditions the captives had endured for what I found out was two months before I came aboard were anything but humane. They were treated as cargo, pure and simple.

The death rate as they sailed across the Atlantic Ocean had been high for both the captives and the ship's crew. Captain Palmer told me that they had lost over 100 slaves and six crewmen. The body count would have been higher had the *Desire* been a "tight pack" ship. Palmer insisted that his cargo be "loose packed" in hopes of reducing the mortality rate. That meant he would be transporting about two-thirds of the number that a tight packed ship could carry.

As we approached port, Palmer confided in me that he abhorred slavery itself – but also that he recognized the economic value of the trade. It was quite lucrative and had allowed him to purchase the *Desire* from its previous owner, who had used it to transport sugar cane, rum, and molasses from the West Indies to the English colonies in America. Palmer explained that the Portuguese and Dutch plantation owners demanded premium prices that could only be offset by larger cargoes. "The colonists are damn stingy with their money," he said as he spat over the railing and raised his spyglass.

"Mister Hailey, ten degrees left rudder if you please!"

"Aye, Sir… Helmsman, set your course ten degrees to port."

"Ten degrees to port, aye."

I was beginning to understand the traditions of command as they had come to exist in the United States Navy of my day. The delivery and acknowledgment of orders I had just witnessed was no different than what I would have done in my last command aboard the *USS Bataan* over three centuries later. Orders were given and acknowledged unambiguously, and I took comfort knowing that the crew was disciplined and efficient.

"Land Ho!" the upper lookout bellowed. From his elevated position near the top of the foremast, he naturally would be the first seaman to see land. "Sir, I can see smoke rising from the villages; I believe it is New Haven, Sir."

Tibbs, the seaman in the "crow's nest," as it was affectionately known, had sailed into New Haven several times previously. He was among the most experienced of the crew and in line to become a merchant officer as soon as a position opened up through death or resignation. Already with ten years before the mast, Tibbs was respected by his shipmates and the informal leader of his watch.

"Very well, Tibbs," Captain Palmer responded.

"Helmsman, continue course," Palmer ordered.

"Continue course, aye," the helmsman responded.

Captain Palmer escorted me forward and asked that I remain there as forward lookout while the *Desire* entered port. My orders were simple: call out any hazards before they hit the *Desire*'s hull. I knew from my own naval training that lookouts were essential to successful docking and anchoring maneuvers.

My mind was racing: here we were in an unpowered vessel with only rudimentary steering and Captain Palmer was going to slide it up to the wharf as if he had side thrusters and twin screws. He was totally confident that he would be able to dock his ship safely; the alternative was to anchor in the harbor and ferry small groups of slaves ashore in rowed longboats. That was a situation Captain Palmer wished to avoid at all costs as he had observed more than one longboat being taken over by the captives, with the eventual loss of all hands – including the oarsmen.

Docking was done with precision and discipline. The *Desire* sidled up to the wharf and was made fast to the stanchions. The crew quickly climbed the masts and made the sails fast to the booms. The whole process took less than an hour.

"Mister Harris!" Captain Palmer bellowed. "Will you accompany me ashore to the public house and a wee draught of ale?"

I could think of nothing finer after the weeks at sea in two different timelines. "Of course, Captain Palmer. It would be my honor to celebrate your seamanship and the safe arrival of the *Desire*."

Chapter Four: Missing, Presumed Dead
Annapolis, July 2015

The strains of the hymn "Eternal Father, Strong to Save" echoed through the nave of the Naval Academy Chapel and could be clearly heard in the crypt of John Paul Jones in the catacomb below. Bethany Harris, Commander, United States Navy (Retired), sat in the front pew. Seated with her was the Academy Superintendent, Vice Admiral William Cartwright, who had been a classmate and roommate of Jonathan Harris during and after their four years at the Academy. The Harrises had no children of their own, were both only children themselves, and all four of their parents had passed away some years earlier. Bethany was glad that her husband's dearest friend was there to provide emotional support.

While they were on active duty, Bethany Harris had accepted the likelihood that her husband could be killed in military operations. She had not been prepared for his sudden disappearance from the yacht he had inherited from his wealthy father. It was as if her whole world had suddenly imploded on her, collapsing like a black hole so dense that no life would ever get out again. Up to this point, she had remained stoic in her grief, keeping everything inside and out of public display.

"C'mon, Chaplain... get on with it!" she thought to herself, her grimace showing the frustration she was feeling. The incessant reading of the citations accompanying her husband's medals and awards was grating on her. She knew Jonathan was a great man; she didn't need the chaplain's stentorian tones to tell her that. She wanted nothing more than to go to the nearest bar and get totally drunk; if Admiral Cartwright wanted to join her in commiseration, that was fine with her.

At the end of the service, the small memorial table was wheeled ceremoniously down the aisle to the narthex. Bethany followed close behind, taking Cartwright's arm for support. His staff car, a bulletproofed SUV, was parked at the base of the chapel stairs, where the two waiting Marines gently loaded the memorial to their missing comrade in arms into the rear cargo area and made it fast.

The Admiral's driver, a Chief Petty Officer, greeted them with a sharp salute as he opened the door. Admiral Cartwright helped Bethany into the back seat, then went to the other side of the car and got in.

"Bill, where are you taking me?" Bethany asked.

"I felt that you… we… need closure. Jonathan is missing and presumed dead," Cartwright responded. "We are going out on my launch with the wreath from the memorial service. Together, we will set the wreath free in the currents going out into the Chesapeake Bay and say goodbye to Jonathan. As luck would have it, we are hitting a strong outgoing tide and the confluence of currents from the Severn and West Rivers should take Jonathan's memorial quickly out into the main bay."

Bethany didn't need the Admiral's "mansplaining." She was a competent mariner in her own right and fully aware of the tides and currents out of Annapolis. *"After all,"* she thought to herself, *"one of our first trips on Jonathan's inherited yacht was from the renowned 'ego alley' across the small harbor from the Naval Academy's docks."* The memory of that first night afloat, anchored several miles south of Annapolis, brought a wistful, but brief, smile to her face.

Dockside, in the Academy's Santee Basin marina, they were met by another pair of smartly uniformed Marines. There was also a four-man rifle squad and its Gunnery Sergeant standing at parade rest next to the seawall.

Bethany was puzzled. *"What is happening here?"* she wondered to herself.

"Commander Harris, would you please come aboard my launch?" Admiral Cartwright said, suddenly changing to a more formal tone. There were, after all, enlisted Marines well within earshot and Cartwright was big on decorum and ceremony. The Marines snapped sharply to attention as she and the Admiral passed by.

Bethany stepped aboard, declining Cartwright's offer of his arm to assist her. "For fuck's sake, Cartwright, I can take care of myself, dammit," she mumbled just loud enough for the Admiral to hear. The last thing she wanted was to show any signs of weakness or emotion in front of the Marines. Women in the Armed Services had come too far, and she was determined that not even the death of her servicemember spouse was going to change her impenetrable façade. Once Bethany was aboard, she donned the military-issue PFD that was required by Navy regulations for all passengers on boats of this type, even the Admiral. She knew the regulations.

The same Chief Petty Officer who had driven them the short distance to the yacht basin was also the pilot of the Admiral's launch. The Chief was assisted by a Bosun's

Mate assigned to the yacht basin. The Chief quickly started the diesel engines, the Bosun's Mate casted off all the lines, and the yacht was gently motored out into the Severn River, the Admiral's three-star flag luffing in the breeze from a short stern staff. The memorial wreath hung from a stanchion on the port gunwale and Bethany was fixated on Jonathan's official photograph in the middle. She suddenly felt the tears welling up and spilling down her cheeks; she wiped them away as an unwanted inconvenience.

After about five minutes, the Chief cut the engines and allowed the vessel to drift in the current. Had it been a weekend, the waters would have been roiling with recreational boating traffic. Being a Thursday, there was next to no recreational traffic and the sea state was nearly calm.

Admiral Cartwright leaned to Bethany Harris's ear. "Are you ready?"

"Yes, Bill. I am… let's get this over with." She trembled as she spoke, and her voice wavered.

"Attention on deck!" Admiral Cartwright ordered. On shore, the rifle squad's Gunnery Sergeant brought the squad to attention, then to firing positions.

Cartwright ordered, "Present Arms!" and snapped a sharp salute along with the Chief. The Bosun's Mate piped the "Last Pipe" call.

"Ten-HUT!" the Gunnery Sergeant bellowed on shore. The sound of heels clicking together in unison was impressive.

Seeing that Bethany Harris was lowering the wreath over the side, the Marine barked, "Ready!" The four well-practiced Marines snapped the butts of their rifles to their shoulders, precisely in unison.

Just as the wreath touched the water, the Gunnery Sergeant barked again, "Fire!"

The simultaneous report from four Garand M-1 rifles startled Bethany Harris. She visibly jumped at the first volley, losing her balance and nearly falling overboard; Cartwright's quick response grabbing her by the PFD harness was the only thing that saved her from a swim in the brackish water of Chesapeake Bay.

"Ready… Fire!" the Marine barked. Again, the shots rang out. Once more, Bethany jumped, but retained her balance.

"Ready... Fire!" the Marine ordered for the final volley. The sound echoed back from the Naval Research Labs across the river and then all was silent. For the first time, Bethany Harris cried tears of grief. This was it. Her husband's final opus. The end of the line. It was now her time, time to begin a new life without her beloved husband.

Her tears quickly devolved into abject hysteria. Completely oblivious to anything around her, Bethany fell to her knees on the hard safety-textured deck and wailed loudly. Her knees were abraded from the fall and oozed blood, but she had no sensation of pain. As her hysteria deepened, she balled herself into a fetal position and wailed even more loudly. She later recounted to a friend that it "was the most undignified thing I had done since high school."

The memorial wreath quickly caught the current and began floating away from the Admiral's launch. "Take as long as you need, Bethany," Cartwright said in as consoling a tone he could muster. Bethany stood slowly and placed her hands on the gunwale railing. Her shoulders drooped as a wave of nausea swept over her. *I've never gotten seasick in my entire Naval career, and now I get green around the gills?* she thought to herself as she vomited the contents of her stomach overboard. *"Everything must be catching up with me...."*

Five minutes passed, then ten, then fifteen and the wreath was finally nothing more than a speck in the distance. Bethany Harris turned to Cartwright and said, "Bill, I'm ready now. Can we go ashore, please?" She finally had her emotions and thoughts under control.

"Of course," the Admiral replied.

"Chief, take us home," Cartwright ordered.

*　*　*　*　*

In an examination room at Walter Reed Military Medical Center in Washington, DC, forty-eight-year-old Bethany Harris had become quite nervous. The nausea she had experienced at Jonathan's wreath ceremony had continued for the next couple of weeks, resulting in uncontrollable vomiting on several occasions. She was perplexed and wondered if perhaps she had an ulcer or some other digestive disorder. Losing a spouse certainly preyed on the emotions and bodily functions.

"Commander Harris," the young doctor said as he walked into the room with an electronic tablet connected to the hospital's laboratory and patient records systems. "I won't sugar-coat this any more than necessary. I want to be the first to congratulate you… you are pregnant."

"Pregnant? How can that be? My periods stopped nearly a year ago and were irregular for a year before that."

"Sometimes, the body gives one last hurrah and a woman's ovaries release a viable egg before shutting down for good. It's one of those unexplained mysteries of the human female body," the young Lieutenant explained. "Just out of curiousity, did you have mumps after puberty?"

"I think maybe… but I'm not sure," Bethany replied.

"Clinical studies have suggested a correlation between mumps as a teen and the possibility of early menopause, or even false menopause," the doctor explained.

"But my husband… he's missing and presumed dead. The last time we… had relations… was on our yacht somewhere off the coast of North Carolina, two nights before he disappeared." She allowed a silent moment to fill the room. "That was six weeks ago." Her voice trailed off into silence and she closed her eyes trying to hold back the inevitable tears, the ones that were now coming at the most inopportune times. At least now she had an explanation of why her emotions were always on edge. It wasn't grief after all! It was the hormone rush that accompanied early pregnancy.

Bethany was unprepared for the news she had been given. It was as if someone had gut-punched her, then did it again as she gasped for breath. She was going to be a mother, whether she liked it or not. The other alternative – abortion – was unthinkable.

*   *   *   *   *

Bethany's memory of her last night with Jonathan was as vivid in her mind as if it had happened only the night before. They were naked and alone on the foredeck of the *Great Escape*. The calm sea was almost glass flat, allowing the unattended use of the autopilot. Before disrobing and heading out to the foredeck, Jonathan made sure alarms were set to alert them if any vessels were detected on radar within five miles, giving them ample time to respond and take evasive action if necessary.

The Lattimores, being a little more reclusive about their marital activities, had retired to their stateroom a couple of hours earlier. The two couples were close enough friends that they did not feel the need to suppress anything and regularly joked about how frequently they all had sex. Had anyone been in the passageway outside the Lattimore's stateroom, it would have been obvious what was happening inside: Virginia Lattimore was quite vocal when she was engaged in such activity.

It was just Jonathan and Bethany on the foredeck in the light of a full moon, accented by the bioluminescent plankton floating on the surface of the water. There was a following breeze; its velocity was the same as their forward progress, giving the illusion of dead calm on the deck. However, their passion was anything but calm and neither of them wanted the lovemaking to end. Though they were both in their forties, they had learned over time what pleased the other.

During their naval careers, they were often apart for weeks or months at a time. Since their retirements, though, their lovemaking had reached new levels, more passionate and erotic than any other time in their marriage. They now had the luxury of time to fully enjoy each other's bodies.

*   *   *   *   *

The memory of their last night together was quickly put out of Bethany's head by the doctor clearing his throat. "Commander Harris, because of your advanced maternal age, we will be treating this as a high-risk pregnancy. Do you live here in the Washington area?"

"We... I... have a small apartment in Annapolis. We used to spend most of our time aboard our... Jonathan's... yacht, so there was no need for anything substantial, nor a house and a mortgage." *"I guess that will change now,"* she thought. *"There's no room for a baby in our apartment and I have already put the yacht up for sale."*

"That's good," the doctor replied. "I expect to see you here at our maternity clinic every two weeks. It's good that have kept yourself in tip-top shape. That's the hardest thing for what we call 'geriatric' mothers to understand: there is a direct link between their health and their ability to carry a baby to term. I am glad to see that you will be the exception to what I usually encounter in such cases."

Commander Bethany Harris, United States Navy (Retired), was in a fog of incredulity as she left what was arguably the best military hospital in the United States. Here she was at forty-eight years of age and pregnant. *"Pregnant! I know how it happened,"* she mused, *"but I didn't think it was possible anymore."* She quickly resigned herself to the reality that she would be a mother in a little more than seven months. She only wished that Jonathan could be there to share her joy.

Chapter Five: Market Commodities
New Haven, Late Summer, 1654

I remained on board the *Desire* as it was relieved of its human cargo. The slaves were taken from the ship in coffles of ten. I found the sounds of chains rattling as they walked to be most unnerving. I knew from my discussions with Captain Palmer that these *human beings* would not be sold immediately; they needed ample time to recover from the rigors of an overcrowded ocean crossing.

The slaves were all taken ashore and led to open-air holding areas – which were nothing more than pens like those used to contain livestock. With Captain Palmer's good wishes, I was paid a basic able seaman's wage for my time aboard and dismissed from the Desire. I quickly disembarked and began to seek my bearings in the New Haven of 1654.

In the 20th and 21st Centuries, New Haven was a bustling metropolitan city. New Haven in 1654, originally known as Quinnipiac, was nothing more than a small port that had been supplanted by Boston and New Amsterdam (which would later become New York City). I remembered enough of the city's history and the maps I had studied for our travels, but none of them went back to the mid-17th Century. Even the John Morris House, one of the surviving buildings I had visited with Bethany, would not be built for another twenty years or more.

Everywhere I turned, there was mud and all manner of animal droppings and human waste. The smell combined with that of the mud from the adjacent marshes and created a nauseating miasma that the locals no longer noticed. It was one of those smells that, once experienced, I would never be able to get out of my mind. I didn't think I would ever adapt to such an aroma.

I quickly found a rooming house a couple of streets removed from the harbor. By the standards of the period, it was both clean and palatial. I paid the landlord a month's rent in advance and was given my choice of any of the available rooms on the second floor. I chose a corner room facing the street so that I could observe the hustle and bustle below. The room also afforded me an overlook of the slave holding pens, something else that I wanted to monitor for activity. It was my intent to be present when the slaves from the *Desire* were auctioned.

The other tenants were several seamen awaiting their next voyage, a couple of peddlers, and a preacher,

Reverend Peter Prudden, along with his companion, Jehu Burr. It certainly was an interesting mix. Prudden, I later found out, was from Fairfield, having settled there several years earlier as their pastor. He had come over from England on the *Hector* in 1637 along with several other Connecticut notables.

I knew that the money I had earned on the *Desire* would eventually run out. I would have to find some way of either bartering for subsistence or laboring for wages. The thought of going back out to sea also was a possibility. Any way I looked at it, I was stuck in time. Stuck in the 17th Century. I had no idea how I had gotten there nor any idea how I could leave and return to my own timeline.

Within a week of my arrival, I witnessed my first slave auction on the New Haven Green. Men and women alike were marched up to the dais in chains and I could see that the group being auctioned had recovered from their weeks at sea. They were spared no indignity as potential buyers inspected each prospective purchase from head to toe. The women's breasts and buttocks were squeezed and fondled, the men's genitals exposed to the crowd, and any imperfections (except for the scars of floggings) were quickly pointed out as bargaining points that might reduce the price to be paid. It was embarrassing for me to watch.

The captives had been kept in the holding pens for about a month before auction. It was customary for the men to be put to work in menial jobs around the town, jobs that none of the Puritan white people wanted to perform. The women generally were assigned to community laundries or gardens. Misbehavior was dealt with very swiftly by the overseers, all of whom carried a coiled leather whip in their belt just like I had seen in First Officer Hailey's belt on the *Desire*.

On the *Desire*, I had expected to see a flogging, but the captive cargo was well-behaved, docile and compliant. I never once saw Hailey remove the whip from his belt. Now ashore, I found myself in the mob that had moved from the auction to a punishment area diagonally across the green.

I quickly recognized the stocks, pillories, and whipping post. There was a white man in the stocks; the sign over his feet said that he was a servant who had tried to run away from his master. In the pillory was a woman who had been accused of witchcraft. Passers-by stopped to spit on her or to dump their spoiled vegetables on her head. I then turned to the whipping post, a rough-hewn post with two iron rings fastened on opposite surfaces.

The mob parted as a lone black man was forcibly marched to the whipping post. As two burly men held him in place, his hands and wrists were fastened to the iron rings. I was fixated on the sight and was startled when I heard the crack of a whip behind me. It was one of the overseers uncoiling his whip and cracking in demonstration that he knew what he was doing. The mob's separation grew as none of them wanted to inadvertently receive a lash from the whip. I asked a man standing next to me why the poor soul was being whipped and all I got in return was a "he probably deserves it" response.

The man winced as the first blow struck him diagonally across his back, from right shoulder to left hip. Blood began to ooze from the raw flesh as the second lash struck in the opposite direction, from left shoulder to right hip. The man did not, as I would have expected, cry out in pain. Instead, he gritted his teeth and flared his nostrils with each blow, which alternated as the first two had done. A whipping such as this was skillfully delivered to inflict maximum pain and leave the most horrific scars, scars which would remind others of the fate that awaited them if they stepped out of line.

I felt tears rolling down my cheeks in sympathy as the final lash was delivered and the man passed out. Twelve lashes in all, each one splaying the man's back almost down to the bone. His back ended up a bloody mess of x-shaped markings. Entertainment over, the crowd quickly dispersed, leaving the beaten man hanging from his wrist bindings. If he was left to hang there too long, it would have the same effect as a crucifixion, leaving him unable to breathe and suffocating.

After a few minutes, a familiar face approached. It was Fatou, the nursemaid from the *Desire*. She was carrying a bundle that I later would learn contained herbal medicines that she had brought all the way from Africa.

Tenderly, Fatou began untying the man. He was dead weight, and I could see that she would not be able to lower him to the ground on her own, so I approached to help her; my actions drew more than a couple of sidelong glances from passers-by. Fatou had, since our last encounter on the *Desire*, learned a few more English phrases.

"Good day, Mister Harris," Fatou said, smiling.

"May I help you, Fatou?" I asked.

"Please, sir," she replied.

Avoiding his shredded and bloody back, I wrapped my arm around his waist as Fatou loosened his bonds. He groaned as his arms fell to his sides. I could tell that he was in a great deal of pain and only had fleeting moments of consciousness.

We laid him face-down on the ground and tucked his arms under his head. Fatou then reached into her bag and pulled out an aromatic poultice; the smell of garlic and fermented cabbage was almost overpowering. Unfolding the linen until only two layers were left, she gently patted it onto the man's wounds. He winced and groaned in pain.

Fatou leaned forward and whispered in the man's ear. I could not understand what she was saying, but I assumed they were words of comfort and encouragement.

She sat back upright and looked at me. "Mister Harris, this man name 'Oumar' and he same village," she explained. Now I understood why she had been so compassionate in her ministrations. It was even possible that they were related in some way.

Fatou called out to the two black men who were walking across the green. By their dress, I could determine that they were freemen and not slaves themselves – but they still understood the African language Fatou was speaking. They came to her aid and took the man between them, draping his arms over each of their shoulders.

"Thank you. Mister Harris," one of the men said in perfect English. "We shall handle the matter from here. It would not be proper for you as a white man to accompany us."

I was speechless and could only nod in agreement as I watched the three men, led by Fatou, stumble off in the direction of the slave pens.

I had been in New Haven for about nine months. Deciding that months away at sea would not be conducive to me possibly finding my way back to the 21st Century, I had signed on to the crew of a local fishing boat as a means of generating some income. It was backbreaking and dangerous work, but like all of the other situations I had encountered since my rescue, I managed to muddle my way through and quickly develop proficiency. I was following the military mindset of "adapt, improvise, and overcome" that is taught in all combat schools, regardless of service.

Mending nets became second nature to me and I found that I enjoyed the precision it required. I would eventually learn that such proficiency was highly admired and sought after. It didn't take long before several captains banded together to secure my services and to make sure I remained on shore to repair one set of nets while they were out to sea with another. Remaining ashore also gave me plenty of opportunities to observe village life and to listen to the gossip of the fishermen's wives.

I was also glad that I could spend most of my working day seated, as I was nearly a head taller than the tallest man in New Haven. The average height of the time was around 5 feet, 7 inches – and here I was at a towering 6 foot 4. Walking down the street, those seeing me for the first time could only stop and stare. The children, normally polite at risk of having their ears boxed, also gawked and pointed. It wasn't every day they saw someone who was nearly a foot taller than their fathers!

The rhythmic and repetitive nature of the work was soothing. Shuttle, twist, knot, repeat. Shuttle, twist, knot, repeat. My carved whalebone shuttle quickly became smooth and shiny from constant use. I felt I had found my 17th Century niche. As long as there was daylight and a nearby fire if the weather was cold, I was able to work. Even rain did not stop my efforts, as I worked under a lean-to shelter next to where the nets were hung to dry between uses.

By the end of the winter, I would be able to charge more for my service. It was an outstanding season for numerous varieties of fish, including wild Atlantic salmon – something that was almost extinct from the East Coast in the 21st Century. The nets and my repair work did not break down under heavy catches and the town would be well-fed through the winter, thanks to the local Natives teaching the colonists how to preserve and dry the fish.

When I wasn't mending the never-ending pile of nets for the fishing fleet, I was seeking whatever information I could find about the Connecticut Colony as it existed in 1655. Unfortunately, newspapers were not yet in circulation, so I had to rely on whatever was posted on the village bulletin board, the town crier, Sunday church services, and word of mouth. Even the Salem Witch Trials were nearly forty years in the future. I could not have ended up in a bleaker period in American history, and at times I wondered when I would wake up from my months-long nightmare.

*   *   *   *   *

On February 17, 2016, Bethany Harris gave birth to a baby boy she named Jonathan Daniel Harris, Junior. Her pregnancy, despite the continual worry of Walter Reed's obstetrics staff, had been uneventful and her labor unusually short for a first-time mother of her age. By her choice, the birth took place without any pain-relieving drugs and Jonathan emerged from the womb with an

APGAR score of 9. He was, despite the statistical odds for such a geriatric pregnancy, remarkably healthy.

Spending only two nights in Walter Reed, Bethany quickly settled into a routine. Being retired with a guaranteed military pension and independently wealthy following the multimillion-dollar sale of the *Great Escape* the previous November, she had paid cash for a home in Edgewater, a suburb south of Annapolis. There, she was able to devote her full attention to young Jonathan and to hire a live-in housekeeper to tackle the domestic tasks she was disinclined to perform.

Wanting to experience motherhood to its fullest after having been denied for so long, Bethany Harris insisted on breastfeeding as her son's only nutrition. With the live-in helper taking care of the rest of the home, Bethany was able to focus totally on infant care and the rigors that breastfeeding entailed. At first, Jonathan demanded a feed every two hours, almost around the clock. Bethany found it exhausting but one of the most fulfilling things she had ever done. Here she was, a woman in her late forties, and successfully breastfeeding a thriving infant. *"This really is a job for younger women,"* she thought, *"but here I am, living the dream!"* She was surprised at the sarcasm in her thoughts.

When baby Jonathan – who Bethany had started calling "JD" not long after his birth – was about three months old and starting to sleep through the night, she was awakened from a deep slumber by a haunting dream. In the dream, she sensed that her husband, Jonathan, was still alive but not able to communicate with her. The only other time in their marriage she had had such a vision was when Jonathan had been badly wounded in combat half a world away.

The dream began repeating itself almost nightly and was so vivid that Bethany eventually began awakening each night confused and disoriented. She had hoped that with JD now sleeping through most nights, she would be able to rest herself. The demands of nursing had exhausted her. *"I don't know how women do this and hold down full-time jobs,"* she remembered thinking. The dreams were taking her rest away from her more than the challenges of motherhood.

In between the seemingly constant feeding and diaper changing, Bethany had been slowly going through her missing husband's personal effects. She had retrieved them for a storage locker in Norfolk, Virginia, not long after she discovered she was pregnant. In the boxes of papers, Bethany discovered a very detailed family tree that tied Jonathan's family to the early days of New Haven, Connecticut. Bethany wondered if her new knowledge of her husband's ancestry was perhaps feeding her subconscious and the dreams that had been more of a disruption to her sleep than caring for JD was.

Bethany had quickly become quite attached and friendly with her live-in. Maria Francesca Rivera Garcia, a legal immigrant from Chile, was a model employee and Bethany made sure that all of the legal entanglements were taken care of. Working through Jonathan's... her... attorney, provisions were made for Maria to pay taxes and to have health insurance. Maria also participated in English language classes for new immigrants and was soaking up the nuances of her new language like a sponge.

Maria recognized that Bethany was having unusual dreams as she had overheard some of the somniloquy a few nights when JD unexpectedly awoke and Maria took him to Bethany's room. Maria eventually suggested that they go to visit a friend of her mother, a legal immigrant living in one of the less trendy areas of Annapolis, who could interpret what Bethany's dreams meant. Bethany was at first skeptical of the whole idea, but Maria had been right about most other things, so Bethany agreed.

Bethany, Maria and JD arrived at the psychic's small home a little after 2 p.m. After making introductions, Maria took JD out of the room and laid him down in his stroller for a nap. He fell asleep almost instantly.

The tiny house was everything Bethany imagined a psychic's parlor would be. A dim lamp with a green shade tasseled in gold gave a soft glow in the center of the room. The perimeter was filled with plants, porcelain dolls, and antique books. The room as a whole was in need of a good dusting; the sunlight coming in through the window illuminated a stream of dust motes so vividly they looked like snow suspended in mid-air. Then there was the mixed pungency of wax candles and the miasma of perfumes that was almost nauseating.

Once they were seated at the small round table, the psychic, Isabella Ava Soto Contreras, looked into Bethany's eyes and took both of Bethany's hands in her own.

"Bethany, I can see you are troubled. Do you know the cause?" Isabella asked in a soothing tone. Isabella's English was almost perfect, with very little accent.

"Yes... I think I do..." Bethany began. "I lost my husband at sea just over a year ago, before I even knew I was pregnant with his... our... first child. I have been on my own since he was declared missing and presumed dead."

'My dear, close your eyes and match your breathing to mine. We need to get you relaxed so I can get a sense of your aura," Isabella instructed. "Did you bring an article with you that belonged to your husband, and a photograph?"

"Yes, I did. I brought his Special Warfare badge. It was his most prized possession when he was in the Navy," said Bethany. "Here's one of our last photographs together, too."

Releasing one of Bethany's hands, Isabella studied the photograph, then took Jonathan's badge and rolled it over gingerly in her palm. Her breathing quickly synchronized with Bethany's. A few moments later, Isabella suddenly gasped as if she had been frightened.

"Bethany, your husband is alive!"

"How do you know that? The Coast Guard declared him 'missing and presumed dead' over a year ago. Where can I find him? Is he okay? Is he hurt?" Bethany's mind was spinning out of control, and she vocalized each thought as it came into her head, each one getting louder and more frenetic than the previous one. The experience was so dizzying that Bethany felt she might faint.

"Please, Bethany, try to be calm. I cannot give you more information yet, and I could easily lose my connection with your husband if you do not control your emotions," Isabella said softly. "The spirits do not like panic."

Isabella needed to get Bethany under control. She had seen situations like this in her many years as a practicing psychic and they usually did not end well. She hoped that Bethany would have the strength to deal with such a revelation, but... not all women maintained their sanity after a revelation that their husband was still among the living. On more than on occasion, Isabella had seen women quickly fall into a catatonic state when she gave them news of their loved one. It was a fine line between reality and insanity.

Isabella Ava Soto Contreras continued, "I am seeing someone from Jonathan's past, perhaps a grandparent or even a great-grandparent, and maybe some fishing boats."

"Jonathan's family originated in Connecticut, but he has no living relatives that I know of," Bethany said with a hint of disappointment in her voice as the images of Jonathan's family tree came into focus in her mind. Even so, she was beginning to think that Isabella was a fraud, a fake, a charlatan. "I think we are done here," said Bethany. "How much do I owe you for your time?"

"Bethany, you have to trust me. The images are not clear, but they are of Jonathan. Of that I am certain," Isabella said with conviction.

"Please, Senora Soto Contreras, let me pay you for your time and leave in peace," Bethany begged. She had decided that using more formal terms of address would drive her point home; she no longer felt that first names were appropriate.

Isabella sensed the shift from casual to formal and adapted her speech as well. "Of course, Mrs. Harris. That will be fifty dollars.".

Bethany reached into her purse and threw three crisp twenty-dollar bills on the table. "Keep the change…" she said with a defiant tone, then roughly snatched the photograph and Jonathan's Special Warfare badge from Isabella's hands.

Out the door in a matter of seconds, Bethany looked to the left and found Maria coming toward her with a giggling JD in the stroller. At the sight of her son and his infectious smile, Bethany almost entirely forgot the session with the psychic – until later that evening, anyway.

Maria put JD to bed at his usual time of 8:00 p.m. and prepared Bethany a cup of herbal tea, then retired to her room. Bethany was alone in the TV area of the open-plan home, watching an on-demand showing of the 1995 movie, "The Scarlet Letter." It was a terrible movie, having earned the distinction as one of the worst films ever made.

In spite of the critical reviews, Bethany was engrossed in the story, having studied Nathaniel Hawthorne's writings in college. However, by the beginning of the second hour of the film, Bethany was fast asleep and quickly reached Rapid Eye Movement, or REM. Her subconscious took her deep into a prolonged dream.

Bethany's previous dreams had been largely without form, including not much more than phantasmic images of Jonathan. This dream, however, was more vivid and lifelike. She sensed she could almost reach out and touch her husband, but like Ebeneezer Scrooge with the three ghosts in "A Christmas Carol," she was nothing more than an observer to the events taking place before her.

Bethany saw that Jonathan was sitting near a small campfire with some sort of needlework in his hands. *"Needlework?"* her unconscious self observed. *"Jonathan never did any needlework in his life that I am aware of. His rudimentary sewing skills were limited to what was necessary to maintain his uniforms and equipment. Nothing more."*

"Jonathan! Don't leave me!" Bethany exclaimed aloud while still deeply asleep. Her outburst was loud enough that it brought Maria running from her room.

"Miss Bethany, are you okay?" Maria asked, gently touching Bethany's arm.

Bethany's eyes were wide with fright. "I think I've seen a ghost…"

Chapter Seven: Cruel and Unusual
The Connecticut Colony, 1655-1656

As time passed, I observed the patterns of life in New Haven and the surrounding villages. Life certainly was simpler in the 17th Century: most people lived and died within ten miles of where they were born. There were, of course, explorers and trappers, itinerant preachers, fishermen and seafarers who ventured far and wide, but they were the exception rather than the rule.

Religion, something that I had never taken seriously even in combat, dominated everyday life. Church attendance was mandatory, and absence could be punished by fines. Old men who fell asleep during sermons were tickled under the chin with feathers. Children who misbehaved could receive public corporal punishment from the deacons. *"So much for their self-esteem,"* I thought to myself.

The legal system, too, was dominated by the church. The Connecticut Colony, founded on the precepts of Puritanism, was no exception. Public whippings were common, as were public executions for venal sins such as adultery or fornication. As I would soon find out, far lesser "sins" went before the lash.

The church was packed for one such trial. It felt odd to me that a church would double as a courthouse, but the idea of a civil administration and the separation of church and state were still a few decades away. At the front of the church, in the area just below the chancel, were seated three men in clerical garb. I recognized immediately that the presiding judge was the Reverend Peter Prudden, from Fairfield. I had met him a few months earlier during my stay at the inn. The other two men, I would later learn, were the Reverend Roger Newton of Farmington, and the Reverend Richard Mather, who had come all the way from Boston.

Over the next three hours, nine witnesses came forward to assert how the defendant, an older, childless housewife, had besmirched their good names.

"Goody Pinkerton told Goody Starbuck that I couldn't cook!"

"Goody Pinkerton told my husband that I spent my day being idle."

It went on and on, with each claim drawing a pearl-clutching gasp from the audience. It was as if the women of the village were playing a 17th Century game of "Can You Top This?" I had to dig my nails into the palm of my hand just to keep from bursting out in laughter a couple of times. It was fortunate for Goody Pinkerton that none of the shrewish harpies had made any accusations of adultery. I shuddered to think what the results of *that* accusation might have been.

After hearing the testimony, Reverend Prudden conferred briefly with the other two judges before he spoke. "Goody Pinkerton, thou hast been found guilty of gossiping and bearing false witness against thy neighbor… Thou hast broken the Eighth Commandment of our Lord, given to the Israelites by Moses in the Book of Exodus. It is the punishment of this court, and the will of God, that thou be taken to the public square, there to receive nine lashes, one lash for each falsehood."

Two burly bailiffs took Goody Pinkerton's arms and frog-marched her down the aisle, out the narthex door, and across the town square. As they left the church, the crowd quickly deteriorated from simple spectators to a howling mob thirsty for blood. As we approached the stocks, pillory, and whipping post, I noticed that a man, dressed in black from head to toe, was already there with a whip at the ready. It almost seemed as if the verdict of the trial had been predetermined.

Goody Pinkerton's arms were stretched overhead and her wrists tightly fastened to the iron rings with rough braided rawhide thongs. I could see that the position of her shoulders would quickly become uncomfortable, then intolerably painful and add to the misery she was soon to suffer. To be sure she did not escape from her bonds, the rawhide was soaked with water, which quickly caused the knots to be slip-proof.

I expected the flogging to begin once the poor woman was secured to the whipping post. That was not to be. With a leering grin, the more corpulent of the two bailiffs leaned inappropriately close to the poor woman's ear and whispered something that I could not hear. From her expression, it was likely that his breath was probably quite vile.

While still closer to Goody Pinkerton's torso than he should have been, the bailiff reached up to the collar of her shift. Using his teeth and letting his foul drool run down her neck and spine, he bit through the edging and tore the garment in two down the center of her back. Had her arms not been secured overhead, it is likely that she would have been rendered quite topless and exposed.

"Goody Pinkerton," the Reverend Prudden's stentorian voice bellowed, "dost thou repent of your sins before God and the people of New Haven?"

"Everything I said was the truth, Reverend. I shall neither recant nor repent," she hissed.

"Then let the flogging begin," Prudden responded as he nodded ceremoniously to the man dressed in black.

The whipsman brought his tool of pain backward, making a resounding "crackl!" The crowd gasped in unison. A second time and Goody Pinkerton winced in anticipation of the pain that was to follow. Her eyes were wild with fear.

Seeing that the first lash was imminent, the crowd suddenly went silent. As the whip whooshed forcefully towards the poor woman's exposed back, it was as if it was splitting the air itself. Just before impact, the skilled whipsman pulled back so that the frayed end of the braided rawhide whip cracked and made its first mark. A bloodless red welt quickly appeared over Goody Pinkerton's right shoulder blade, looking like a large welt from an insect bite. I could see he was teasing her and taking sadistic pleasure in administering her punishment. He repeated the same technique on her left shoulder blade. Two lashes down, seven to go.

The next lash brought the full force of the whip across her back, from left shoulder to right hip. Goody Pinkerton howled in pain. It was a loud, guttural scream so woeful and gut-wrenching that I began to tremble out of empathy. Her delicate skin was split almost immediately from the harsh stroke and blood welled up before running down the poor woman's back, quickly staining her white shift.

With Goody Pinkerton now screaming and thrashing like a wounded banshee, the whipsman delivered the fourth lash. It cracked across her exposed torso in the opposite direction, making a bloody "X" on her back. Four lashes down, five more to go.

The fifth lash was delivered in the same direction as the third, but the skill of the whipsman brought the blow about three inches further down her back. This made it possible for the last couple of feet of rawhide to wrap around Goody Pinkerton's torso and her left breast. As blood began to ooze from the fresh wound on her side, Goody Pinkerton passed out, her body falling limp in her bonds. She remained unconscious for the remainder of her beating. With the next blow, the crowd began to disperse; they had lost interest once the poor woman lost consciousness and control of her excretory functions. She was now bleeding *and* soiled.

"Man, this is some serious shit," I mused silently as I observed my first public flogging of a white person, and a woman at that! I had seen the slave being flogged months before and the threats of similar punishment on board the *Desire*, but never did I envisage that a woman would receive the same harsh punishment. *"Cruel and unusual punishment… it certainly doesn't fit the crime."*

I couldn't help but feel sorry for her and wanted to take her down from the whipping post. But… if I did, it would be up to me to take care of her and to clean and dress her wounds. I had seen plenty of wounded men and women in combat, but I realized that I had no stomach for the torture this poor woman had endured. I also remembered the promise I had made to my wife when we were first married that I would tell her every detail of any encounters I had with female warriors that involved any sort of close personal contact. This would have been one of those situations, and I still had not reconciled myself to the fact that I was no longer in the same timeline with Bethany – so I kept my distance for the moment.

I felt as if I had the proverbial angel and devil dancing on opposite shoulders. The angel kept telling me that I should help the poor woman. The devil, prodding me in the neck with his pitchfork, reminded me that I would be violating Bethany's trust and that I should just leave Goody Pinkerton to fate.

As Goody Pinkerton hung there unconscious, a cawing murder of crows drew me out of my stupor. They were hopping closer and closer to Pinkerton's limp and broken body, likely drawn by the scent of her blood, perspiration, and traumatic incontinence. One of the crows tentatively pecked at her ankle, then jumped away in anticipation of a response. Another crow alighted on top of the whipping post and made a similar probe of her fingers and the crown of her head. I laughed out loud that someone had decided that "murder" was the proper name for a group of the black tricksters. A murder of crows, indeed.

The angel on my right shoulder finally won out. I had to do something to help this woman, my pact with Bethany be damned. Taking the fisherman's knife from my belt, I approached the post, gently encircled her waist with my left arm, and cut the rawhide bonds. She fell limply into my arms with an involuntary groan of pain.

Because of the wounds to her back, I quickly maneuvered her inert form into a firefighter's carry, like I had been taught in my various warfighting schools. She couldn't have weighed more than a hundred pounds, which was nothing for an in-shape military man, retired or not, to carry quite a long distance. I knew immediately that my next stop would have to be the slave pens, where I could find Fatou and hopefully get some help for the poor woman.

At the slave holding area, I quickly found Fatou. Because she was owned by a benevolent merchant and had special status as a healer, she was allowed to come and go as she needed. That was fortunate as neither of the two physicians in New Haven wanted anything to do with treating slaves. It naturally fell to Fatou to minister to the slaves' needs. It was also Fatou who provided care to people like Goody Pinkerton after they had been administered their punishments. No physician would touch them either, for fear of running afoul of the ecclesiastical judges or the townspeople.

"Fatou, this poor woman has been whipped and needs your help," I pleaded.

"Yes, Mister Harris. I saw it all. I can help you take care of her," Fatou replied. Her English had improved even more since the last time I saw her, after the male slave had been beaten several months earlier.

"What do we need to do?"

"First, we clean her wounds. Rum, maybe…"

"And after that?"

"A salve of honey and ground Indian saffron will stop infection and help healing."

"Let's get on with it, then."

Over the next few minutes, Fatou tenderly ministered to Goody Pinkerton. She regained consciousness for a few moments as the first medicine was applied, then swooned once more, probably from the mind-numbing pain. Fatou assured me that this was normal for someone in Goody Pinkerton's condition. "I see even grown men do the same thing," Fatou assured me. "They all live."

At this point, I had no idea what I was going to do with the Pinkerton woman. Given the Puritan moral standards, it would not be appropriate for me to take her back to my meager accommodation which was nothing more than a thatched roof hovel enclosing a cot and cooking fire. I had also learned from listening to the crowd at her beating that her husband, Joshua Pinkerton, was a trapper. He was gone for months at a time and was not expected to return before the first snowfall – which was still several weeks away.

Fatou somehow sensed my dilemma. "Mister Harris, I have spare cot in my room. Goody Pinkerton stay with me until she better."

"Fatou, I thank you so much."

*　　*　　*　　*　　*

It took over a week for Goody Pinkerton to regain coherency. She endured multiple fevers despite Fatou's attentive care and repeated salving. Being the curious person I was, I checked in with Fatou every day to see how the poor woman was doing. With each visit, Fatou assured me that everything that was happening was perfectly normal and that I should not worry.

"Why was I so concerned with the wellbeing of this woman?" I asked myself. *"Was I that desperate for female companionship that I would allow sympathy and empathy*

to override logic? What about Bethany? Would I ever see her again?" My mind raced.

Through all my years of military service while married to Bethany, I had never strayed. There were opportunities, yes, but none tempting enough that I would cross that imaginary line in the sand that I always saw in three dimensions. Bethany was my everything and without her, I was incomplete.

At the end of the second week, Fatou had no choice but to release Goody Pinkerton from her care. Still weak and sore, the Pinkerton woman stumbled out of Fatou's makeshift clinic and walked straight towards me.

"I thank you, Mister Harris, for your kind attention. I do not deserve to be treated so kindly after what I was convicted of," she said, her pleasant and slightly musical voice barely audible.

"Goody Pinkerton, it is what any human being *should* have done," I replied. "Would you like something to eat other than Fatou's special broth?"

Chapter Eight: Ghosts in the Graveyard
New Haven, 2017

It took two full days for Bethany to drive herself, JD, and Maria from Maryland to New Haven. It was, for the most part, a comfortable trip in Bethany's brand-new Lincoln Navigator. Normally, such a drive could have been made in a single day. However, Bethany was still nursing JD and that slowed the trip down considerably. Maria was not yet licensed to drive, and even if she was, nursing while underway was not safe for either mother or baby. JD was on limited solid foods, but Bethany was reluctant to completely wean him from the breast. That meant stopping at somewhat regular intervals.

Reaching New Haven just before sundown on the second day, the trio checked into a mini-suite in a mid-grade hotel on the waterfront with no end date for their occupancy. Bethany made sure the room had a view of the harbor and waterfront; she was certain that her dream involving Jonathan a few days earlier was somehow connected to the water and maybe the ocean. She needed to deduce what that connection was.

Bethany wandered aimlessly around New Haven for several days. She visited the New Haven Historical Society, nearly every pre-Revolutionary cemetery, and most of the churches that had links to the early history of the city. There were lots of Harris property transactions, tombstones and church records. She wondered how she would, how she could connect them all to her beloved Jonathan. It certainly wasn't going to be easy.

Finally pulling out the handwritten family tree she had discovered in Jonathan's personal effects, she visited New Haven's oldest cemetery once more. Most of the older gravestones had eroded into unreadability, but one – in a Harris family plot, no less – appeared like a lightning bolt. The names and dates matched similar information on the family tree:

Here lies Jonathan Harris

Born in Virginia

Died July 1658

Loving Father of Benjamin Harris

Bethany felt as if she had been poleaxed from behind. She dropped immediately to her knees as she reached out to touch the gravestone, though it was more of a caress than a touch. Here was an individual almost four centuries earlier that was definitely one of Jonathan's ancestors.

As Bethany knelt at the gravestone, she felt a presence come over her. It was what she had felt after the vivid dream that compelled her to travel to New Haven. She sensed that her missing-and-presumed-dead husband was somehow nearby.

"It isn't possible or logical," she said to Maria. "I feel as if Jonathan is right here with me."

"I told you my mother's friend was a real psychic," Maria responded, the tone of her voice surprising Bethany.

"I guess I should not have let my disbelief get in the way of what Isabella was telling me," Bethany said dejectedly.

Looking around for a few more minutes, Bethany located what she believed to be Benjamin Harris's gravestone. It was, as was customary for the period, considerably smaller than his father's and of a lower-quality stone. Most of the dates had weathered away except for the year of death, 1660. The inscription below the name probably was "Beloved Son" or something similar – but like the dates, it had weathered almost into oblivion. Bethany guessed, knowing the conditions of the period, that the young Benjamin probably died of a childhood malady that would have been preventable in her century..

Once Bethany regained her composure, they left the cemetery and entered the grounds of the nearby church. It was Wednesday, so it was likely that someone would be in the nearby church office building that might have access to the church's historical records that consisted of birth, baptism, marriage, and burial records. She noticed the cornerstone on what appeared to be the oldest part of the building: "1645."

Confronting the church secretary, Bethany became quite demanding.

"I need to see your records from about 1650 to 1660. It is an urgent matter," Bethany demanded.

"How can something nearly four hundred years ago be so urgent?" the secretary replied sarcastically.

"My husband has been missing for almost two years. The Navy has even declared him dead. Somehow, though, I think your records might be connected to him. Please will you show me the congregation's archives?" Bethany pleaded.

"It is time for my lunch break," the secretary noted as she looked at her watch. Bethany realized immediately that this woman had no interest in helping her. "Come back at 1:30," the secretary said coldly as she ushered Bethany and Maria to the outside door. Once the two interlopers were outside, the secretary emphatically locked the door and turned away. Bethany was puzzled by the way the woman blushed when she talked about her lunch break.

"Damn that woman," Bethany said to no one in particular. "She was no more interested in helping than I am interested in the price of wheat in Missouri."

"Miss Bethany," Maria said, trying to console her employer, "we should do as this woman says and be outside this door again at 1:30. We, too, need some lunch and..." she paused to sniff the air, "JD is in need of a diaper change."

"Thank you, Maria, for always looking out for me. You are more to me than just a domestic help. You are a true friend," said Bethany as she took Maria's hand with tears welling up both of their eyes.

The awkward moment now passed, Maria said, "Let's try the café around the corner. It looked quite interesting."

"You usually have a good eye for things, Maria. I am right behind you," Bethany replied.

Over their lunch of frittatas and empanadas, Bethany talked nonstop about her strategy for researching Jonathan's ancestors. First, they would find the burial record for the headstone, then backtrack through the records to find the 17th Century Jonathan's parents. "It will be a slow process," Bethany said. "The handwriting of that century can be difficult to decipher, unless the records were transcribed into typewritten pages." She hoped the latter would be true for this parish as well. It was a very small and almost financially insolvent church, so it was highly unlikely its congregation had devoted any funds for records preservation, short of a benefactor willing to underwrite the expense.

Bethany suddenly realized that she had the wherewithal to hire an archivist and a historian specializing in 17th Century penmanship. She would not let the church's financial situation stand in her way. It was quickly becoming her quest and her obsession to find out as much about the Harris ancestors as she could. Where the chase would lead was still a mystery.

The church secretary did not return until almost 2:00 p.m and did not offer any excuses for her tardiness. Observing that the woman's make-up was now smudged and her clothing in wrinkled disarray, Bethany stifled a chuckle as she realized the woman had experienced a little "afternoon delight" during her lunch hour.

"I see you came back," the secretary said, re-stating the obvious. "Now... what can I do for you?"

"I am a woman of means," Bethany began, "and I am guessing that your church records are still in their original handwritten format and have never been transcribed into a more modern type of record. I would like to hire an archivist, a genealogist, and a historian from Yale University to assist me with both my research and the preservation of your parish's documents."

"I will have to ask the Reverend," replied the secretary. She recognized that Bethany meant business and that the plan to hire the two specialists was going to happen with or without the Reverend's assent. She turned and went to the pastor's study, which was tucked into a corner out of sight of the entry door.

"Reverend Mather, there is a woman in the outer office, a Mrs. Bethany Harris, who is demanding access to our historical records. She is even willing to hire a team of researchers to help preserve our records… What should I tell her?"

"Mrs. Appleton, you know as well as I do that the history of this parish is perhaps more important to outsiders than it is to our members. Remember where I came from? My name, Mather, is closely tied to the history of New England and notably the Salem Witch Trials. The Reverends Increase Mather and Cotton Mather are in my family tree, and I would not have known this without poring over the archives of more than one parish, this one included. Please make it possible for Mrs. Harris to do as she wishes; I can provide contacts at both Yale and Harvard who can help with her endeavors."

"Of course, Reverend," Mrs. Appleton replied. She turned and went back to the outer office.

"Mrs. Harris, Reverend Mather has given his permission for you to have unrestricted access to our historical records. He agrees that your hiring a team of academics is in the best interest of this parish and our records, assuming, of course, that you are willing to make a donation to our preservation fund. Would you like me to provide you with a list of our contacts at Yale and Harvard?"

Bethany could not believe the change in Mrs. Appleton's attitude and demeanor. She had evolved from a perfunctory gatekeeper to a sympathetic assistant in the matter of a few short hours. *"Perhaps it was her extended nooner that changed her tune?"* Bethany wondered to herself, a smirk spreading across her face.

Chapter Nine: Recovery
New Haven, Winter, 1656-1657

Goody Pinkerton, whose Christian name I found out was Dorcas, made a full recovery from the whipping. Fatou had worked miracles with her African herbal treatments, telling me that the scars across Dorcas's back were nothing more than red lines that would fade into white over time. Fatou also told me that if Dorcas would eat more and put on some weight, the scars would fade even more.

I had to base my assessment on Fatou's words, as it would not have been proper for me to examine the bare back of a woman who was not my wife, nevermind what she had publicly suffered at the whipping post. The mores of Puritan colonial Connecticut were a far cry from the public display of skin that I had become accustomed to in my 20th and 21st Century lifetime. In some respects, the formality of my current timeline seemed more polite and honorable than what we would consider to be normal over three and a half centuries years later.

With winter approaching, Dorcas Pinkerton expected her husband, Joshua, to return any day. She knew that he would have been working traplines along the Hudson River valley, heading as far north as possible before turning south to stay ahead of the snowfall. Beaver and river otter pelts were always in high demand for shipment back to England; the aristocrats and gentry there would pay premium retail prices to their suppliers in London, but none of that markup was ever passed on to the trappers in the wild. It was still a lucrative line of work, though the purchasing agents in the colonies intentionally deflated prices or reduced the price per pelt because of alleged imperfections that "His Lordship simply would not tolerate."

By Christmas of 1656, Joshua Pinkerton had not returned to his home and Dorcas began to worry for his safety. I couldn't tell if she truly loved the constantly absent trapper or if she was simply satisfied that she was married to a man who was able to provide for her. The customs of the period treated marriage as more of a business arrangement than a loving relationship, and Dorcas was somehow in the middle of the two.

As 1656 rolled into 1657, I met Dorcas in the village square. It was a crisp but sunny day, with temperatures well above freezing. She was sitting on a bench outside the general merchant's shop which doubled as a post office of sorts. Mail from outlying areas would be dropped off there and the residents of nearby homes and businesses would drop by several times a week to pick up their correspondence from elsewhere in the colonies or from England. There was usually a line outside the door when a ship arrived from England, as most of New Haven still had family there.

As I got closer, I could see that Dorcas was weeping, a letter clutched between her hands.

"Goody Pinkerton," I called out, using the formality that was necessary because of the distance between us, "what troubles you so?" "*I'm starting to sound more like them every day,*" I thought.

"Mister Harris, please sit down," she asked, patting the bench next to her. "I just received a letter from a trapper far up north. He claims that my husband, Joshua Pinkerton, is dead. He froze to death when the weather suddenly turned cold."

This revelation brought on another bout of weeping, something that even in my military years would make me weak at the knees. Women crying always had a weird effect on me, and it took lots of practice for me to control my own emotions to make rational decisions or give orders in times of stress, especially when female sailors were involved. The Navy of my day truly was genderless, with women filling jobs in every possible rating, Special Warfare included.

Despite the impropriety of the situation, I felt compelled to take Dorcas Pinkterton into my arms and hold her close to my body to comfort her. It was awkward for me, as I dreamed of Bethany almost nightly – but it was also the first time I had been physically and emotionally close to a woman since before I was taken aboard the *Desire* a year and a half earlier. The vivid memories of my last night with Bethany, naked on the foredeck of the *Great Escape* also haunted me and woke me from a deep sleep on more than one occasion with an obvious physical response more appropriate for a teenage boy than a man nearing middle age.

My dreams notwithstanding, I was tempted to kiss Dorcas as we stared into each other's eyes but thought better of crossing that line as we were in a very public place. Before I could consider such an affront, she would have to announce her husband's demise in church on Sunday morning and endure a mourning period that would last until spring. Until then, it would not be proper for her to consort with a man that was not a relative. I could not, under Puritan strictures, give her any aid, comfort or advice until the mourning period had passed.

A few days later, after the Sunday morning announcement, we met again.

"Mister Harris…"

I interrupted her before she could say another word. "Please call me Jonathan when we are alone."

"Of course, Mister… uhh… Jonathan… I must tell you that my husband was a good provider for me and always left me enough money to purchase food and supplies while he was away. The one thing, I am embarrassed to admit, is…" she paused to look conspiratorially around before continuing, "that he could not father children. After our wedding night, he lost his ability to… well… there was an accident with a horse."

"Say no more, Dorcas. I know exactly of what you speak." The poor chap had the 17th Century equivalent of irreversible erectile disfunction! The poor woman… I understood what she was telling me: she wanted and needed a romp in the sack.

"Dorcas, I appreciate your confiding in me – but what am I to do about it? We are not married and if you were to get with child, well… if we were to be caught, we would both be taken before the court. What I understand from common law is that it would be considered fornication, and I fear that the punishment would be severe. You are newly widowed, and I am an outsider, having been rescued at sea."

"Jonathan, it matters not to me what other people think. They knew my husband was incapable… I told them so… and it may have embarrassed them enough that they brought the charges against me last year. They didn't want to hear any more about what was happening or perhaps not happening in our bed."

I could not fault Dorcas Pinkerton's logic. She was thinking more like a woman of my century than one who had been born into the 17th Century. I also suddenly realized that the gossiping she had been accused of was actually what the other nine so-called witnesses had been doing all along. It was those women, not Dorcas, who should have suffered the pain of the lash. Instead, they had all conspired against Dorcas to cover their own calumny.

*　*　*　*　*

Spring came early to New Haven in 1657. The snow was all but gone by the middle of March, almost a month earlier than usual. It meant the end of Dorcas Pinkerton's mourning and gave her the freedom to do as she wished. She wasted no time pursuing me as a suitor and began spending nearly every waking moment with me on the wharf where I was repairing the fleet's nets. There were subtle touches, caresses across my shoulders, beaming smiles, and plenty of food delivered to my lean-to. *"My, this woman can cook!"* I thought. *"Bethany... well... never quite got the hang of cooking."*

A guilty feeling rose from the pit of my stomach. I was now comparing Bethany to Dorcas, and not favorably, either. Was I losing touch with the memory of my dear wife of the 20th and 21st Centuries? Or was it simply human nature and acceptance of my current situation taking over? I could not reconcile that concept in my own mind and the guilt followed me night and day for several weeks. During that time, I did everything I could to discourage Dorcas's advances, but my resistance was certainly wearing thin.

Chapter Ten: Staying
New Haven, 2018

The research at the New Haven church took longer than anyone anticipated. The information held in the archives were more extensive than anyone could have imagined. It even included a list of a small band of Quinnipiac Indians who had converted to Christianity and had been baptized. Bethany was left with no choice than to take a short-term lease on a nearby two-bedroom apartment so that she could oversee the research while still being close to JD and Maria. As was the case with most archivists, historians, and genealogists, they were easily distracted by even the smallest snippet of information and could debate for hours the merits of their arcane discoveries. It fell to Bethany to keep them on task.

With the assistance of Reverend Mather, Bethany had hired Pierre Delacroix, Ph.D., from Harvard as her archivist. Delacroix was a dapper man with a distinguished amount of gray in his full head of hair. His build told of many spare hours spent in physical activities. Bethany was surprised at her reaction the first time she met him. *"He certainly is a handsome man!"* said the voice inside her head.

From Yale, she had hired two more Ph.D.s, August Freitag, as her genealogist and Sarah Krankheit as the historian. They were both the epitomes of bookworms, somewhat overweight and with a pallor that told of countless hours spent indoors with very little natural light. Freitag's jowly face, rheumy eyes, and overly large ears reminded Bethany of a basset hound. Sarah Krankheit, on the other hand, had a certain feline quality – but more of an overweight housecat than one that had spent a lifetime chasing mice. *"I guess I won't be judging these books by their covers,"* she mused internally.

All three of the Ph.D.s had taken research sabbaticals from their universities at full salary, a fact that was not known to Reverend Mather. Bethany merely had to provide them with room and board. Bethany decided to handle it like temporary duty assignments were funded in the military: give them a per diem allowance; how they spent it was entirely up to them. It was a mere coincidence that they all ended up in the same rental accommodations.

About a week into the project, Bethany considered discharging Freitag and Krankheit. It turned out that they at one time had been married to each other. They divorced because, as August so succinctly put it, "Only one of them could be right, and that wasn't her!" Bethany had to again rely on her military training to defuse the situation and keep them from killing each other, literally and figuratively. "You *have to* work together," she told them during a closed-door meeting before dinner one evening, "because you are both the best at what you do. I hope you can see past your differences and realize that we have an opportunity to decipher more of New Haven's history than was ever previously known."

August gave a short nod to Bethany and turned to his ex-wife. "I can if you can, Sarah. We were 'us' such a long time ago and it is time for us to get along as colleagues."

Sarah blushed deeply. She had realized some time ago that she still loved the old coot and really did not want their project to be plagued by the vitriol and dogma that had doomed their marriage. "Of course, August. We will work together on this project."

"Thank you both for agreeing to work together. I was nearly ready to discharge you both," Bethany told them as she ended the meeting. "Now… let's eat!"

Ending the meeting and making sure that newly weaned JD and her *au pair*, Maria, were settled for the evening, Bethany summoned Dr. Delacroix from his room to join the research team for dinner. The four met in the building's lobby before venturing out in search of a suitable eatery. All of them loved seafood, so they settled on an oyster bar near the Pequonnock Yacht Club. At dinner, Bethany insisted that they not discuss their project; rather that they focus on their personal lives and professional history. Bethany wanted it to be a social occasion, but it still took a couple of drinks before the normally reserved trio of academics loosened their tongues.

Sarah Krankheit spoke first. "I did my undergraduate work in history, got a Master of Library Sciences, and then followed with a doctorate in history – all from UConn."

"Impressive!" Bethany replied. "What about you, August?"

"Well… Sarah and I met at UConn while she was working on her MLS. It was a whirlwind romance… maybe I should be calling it a 'whirl-*whim*' romance as we certainly didn't think about what we were doing when we did it," August teased.

Sarah slapped Augusts playfully on the shoulder. "You silly old man…"

"Dr. Delacroix, what about you?" Bethany asked, trying to keep the conversation going.

Of French ancestry, Delacroix grew up in a bilingual household in Quebec. There was just a hint of a residual accent in his speech, which added to his mystique and attractiveness. When she was around Delacroix, she felt a flutter of... well, she wasn't quite sure *what* she was feeling!

Delacroix's answer was more philosophical than the others. "Well... I have spent nearly my entire adult life at Harvard, first as a student, then as a professor, before taking on the position of Chief Archivist. The solitary life of an archivist suits me just fine," he said matter-of-factly. "I cannot see myself in any other situation."

August raised his left eyebrow quizzically. "A man of your standing shouldn't be wasting away in an office or the archives, Harvard or not."

"Dr. Delacroix, did you ever marry?" Bethany asked. It was more than just an attempt at making small talk; she was truly interested in his marital status.

"I have chosen to remain a bachelor. I do not like being dependent on another person nor having that person relying on me. Partnerships outside of situations like our present arrangement, with no common bond other than a research project, just do not suit me. I am better alone." Delacroix's tone was dismissive of people whose personalities became so intertwined with their partner that they transformed into a single entity.

Bethany had some empathy for the learned man's chosen lot in life. As he spoke, she suddenly realized that if she had never fallen head-over-heels in love with Jonathan Harris, they would not be sitting around the dinner table as they were at that moment in time. That also meant she would not have had JD, either, but that was a totally separate issue. *"I can raise a child on my own, no husband required,"* she thought to herself. Bethany had suddenly realized that she was no longer actively grieving the loss of her husband. It was only her curiosity that drove her efforts to discover what might have happened to him. *"Damn you, Jonathan Harris!"*

As the evening went on, drinks flowed freely, resulting in their inebriation before the establishment closed for the night. None of the four were falling-down drunk and walking back to their apartments was more like a wandering amble. Along the way, the four split into two couples, with Sarah and August walking well ahead and out of earshot of Bethany and Pierre. Bethany took notice when Sarah took August's arm and got a little closer to him than would have been appropriate for mere work colleagues. She surmised that the two would be spending the night together and probably not getting much sleep.

Bethany found Delacroix at times tedious and always arrogant, but physically attractive just the same. She had seen similar personality quirks in Jonathan that she later learned were simply a smug confidence and self-assuredness that went along with being a Special Warfare Officer in the United States Navy.

She had been watching Pierre all evening, naturally averting her gaze to avoid making eye contact any longer than was necessary for the conversation. She also wanted to suppress the perception that she was staring. It had been almost three years since her last time with Jonathan and her body ached with desire. Delacroix's striking physical attractiveness was overriding her logic and self-control.

"Control yourself, girl! Don't come across as too eager... it might turn out that he actually would have preferred to be with Jonathan..."

Reaching the apartment building lobby, Pierre Delacroix turned and suddenly took Bethany's hands in his own. "Bethany, I said I was unmarried by choice, but I didn't say that I was a celibate monk…" She blushed a deep crimson at his forthrightness. "I would like it very much if you would join me for a nightcap." His eyes twinkled as he winked and smiled warmly.

Bethany's heart was pounding, and she was suddenly as giddy as a teenager who had just been noticed by the football team's star quarterback. It was not entirely clear what Pierre Delacroix's intentions were, but Bethany was prepared to go along with anything he might suggest.

"Well, almost anything," she mused silently. There were places she certainly would not go, and definitely not on a first encounter. She was also worried about being away from JD overnight, but knew he was in good hands with Maria.

They were barely inside the door of Delacroix's apartment when he swept Bethany into his arms and kissed her passionately. To her own surprise, she did not turn away and made it clear that she was ready for more. She melted into his kiss and probed his mouth with her tongue. His hands slid down to her backside and he pulled her even closer, so close that she could feel… "Oh, my!" she moaned out loud, knowing full well what was about to happen.

Bethany was even more surprised when Pierre picked her up and carried her down the hall to his bedroom. Their clothing flew around the room as it quickly came off and they fell into bed in a writhing heap of arms and legs.

"Three years is a long time and I've waited entirely too long," Bethany thought to herself. She was totally ready for his… "Oh, my God!" she groaned deeply. "Don't stop! Please, Pierre… don't stop!"

Chapter Eleven: Just One Touch
Spring, 1657

Dorcas began sitting in the same pew with me in church on Sunday mornings. At first, we were at opposite ends with four to six other people between us, depending on how well they had been eating. When she thought other people would not notice, she would catch my eye, smile and coquettishly bat her eyelids. My resistance to her obvious advances was wearing thin.

When it was finally warm enough to open the church's windows and spring was obviously in the air, Dorcas began sitting next to me, but not so close as to be inappropriate. Still, I could feel her radiating warmth – or was it my own nervousness with the situation? It was like a jolt of electricity when she bridged the space between us and gently caressed the back of my hand with her fingertips. I hoped no one had noticed my reaction. It was just a fleeting touch, but it spoke volumes.

It also seemed that Dorcas was going out of her way to visit me in the boatyard almost daily, ostensibly under the premise that she was there to buy a fish for supper. When none was to her liking, she would dally at my net mending shack and engage in small talk. I had to be careful that I did not provide her with information that would have been inappropriate for 1657.

"Mr. Harris, what was it like in the Virginia Colony?" Dorcas asked one warm spring day.

"The insects were terrible. It was fortunate that the Indians taught us how to keep them at bay. Bear grease smells horrible to humans, and I guess even more so to the insects as they never bothered me after that," I explained. "Our winters, though, were nowhere near as bad as they are here in the Connecticut Colony. Cold, yes, but not the bitter cold like you have here." I was basing my assessment on the years I had spent in the Tidewater area of Virginia during my naval career.

"I know you were lost at sea and recovered by the *Desire*. Were you a seafaring man with no wife waiting for you at port?" I felt as if I was being interrogated.

I had to stop and think. If I waited too long, Dorcas would think I was being evasive less than truthful. I wanted to tell her that I was once married, perhaps that my wife had died in childbirth. It would be a believable story as many women of her time died in childbirth and their newborns shortly thereafter. I decided that I should use the

114

death-in-childbirth story to explain my marital status. Being a widower was certainly better than being an adulterer or fornicator in the eyes of the devout Puritans of New Haven.

Trying not to interrupt my work, I explained my situation to Dorcas Pinkerton. She listened intently and expressed her condolences for the loss of my wife and newborn son. *"Whew! She bought the story, hook line and sinker,"* said the little voice in my head. *"Now I just have to remember that story line…"*

What happened next was a complete surprise. Dorcas sat down next to me on the elongated bench and took a bobbin from the basket next to my feet. Before I knew what was happening, she had lifted a small net onto her lap and was quickly repairing a large hole with a dexterity that was baffling. I had to stop what I was doing and watch; I am pretty sure that my jaw dropped with incredulity.

"Are you surprised, Mr. Harris… Jonathan?" she asked.

"Yes, Dorcas, I am. It is obvious that you have mended nets before," I observed.

"I may have been a trapper's wife, but my father was a fisherman. My own mother died giving birth to me, and

Father never remarried and raised me on his own. I learned how to mend nets from him."

"Mending nets is certainly an unusual skill for a woman," I noted.

"Yes, it is," she replied, "but I think you already know that I am no ordinary woman."

I certainly was surprised by her assertiveness and confidence. Most women I had observed were totally deferential to their husbands and men in general. Goody… Dorcas Pinkerton was so far from the epitome of New Haven womanhood and certainly not the gossiping harpy she had been punished for allegedly being. I couldn't help but admire her determination and fortitude.

Her dogged personality aside, Dorcas was a strikingly beautiful woman. Well… she had a pretty face, anyway… The rest of her body was covered by modest Puritan attire devoid of any ornamentation. She was the widow of a trapper, and the Puritan dress code did not allow her to wear anything that could be construed as excessive and above her station.

Contrary to the legends I had been taught in my history classes, Puritan dress was not just black and white. I had noticed that women wore more colorful attire during the week, saving their black-and-whites for Sunday services. Dorcas was no different, and usually wore hues of blue, green, or gray. I also knew, from assisting her into Fatou's care after the public whipping, that Dorcas Pinkerton was certainly not overweight and had a figure that would have been flaunted with a bikini in the 20th and 21st Centuries.

As darkness fell on the warm spring evening, we walked from the wharf back to my small hovel of a home, guided by the light of a nearly full moon. During the leisurely stroll, she kept an appropriate distance to avoid any accusations of impropriety. Since her punishment, she had become a social outcast while continually under the watchful eyes of New Haven's religious elders. It would be very difficult for her to make any further physical advances without someone somewhere seeing it.

As we approached my little cottage, Dorcas's head was on a swivel. She was more aware of her surroundings than some of my men and women were in combat under hostile enemy fire. I wondered what she might be looking for; it only took a minute or two before I would find out.

Between my cottage and the shed next door was a darkened passageway, gated at both ends to keep unwanted wildlife or dogs out of the rear garden and chicken coop. As we walked past, Dorcas gracefully opened the outer gate with her right hand, grabbed me with her left, and in one smooth motion pulled me into the passageway. The counterweighted gate closed and latched on its own.

"Jonathan, you may kiss me if you wish," she said softly.

"I do wish to kiss you, Dorcas. I have just been waiting for an appropriate opportunity, and you have presented us with one this evening," I replied.

Our first kiss was tentative, but the ardor of the moment quickly increased. It was as if our shared net mending had been the kindling for a bonfire that radiated heat for a considerable distance. She was the most passionate kisser I had experienced; not even Bethany could come close – and *her* kisses were always enough to make me weak at the knees.

Dorcas Pinkerton was not just a wonderful kisser, but also very demonstrative with how much further she wanted things to go. She loosened her overshawl and guided my hand to her still-covered breast, kissing me even more deeply as my caress found her erect nipples through the coarse material of her dress and bodice.

118

"Jonathan, I have been without a man's attention for a long time. I already told you the story of how my husband was injured and unable to… fuck me… like a husband should."

I was surprised at her very direct choice of words. I knew the word had been around for many centuries but wasn't prepared to hear it coming from a Puritan woman's mouth. Perhaps her saltiness was the result of being brought up by her father; regardless, I was not complaining. I had always favored a direct approach and direct language. It was unambiguous what she wanted and needed, and I was going to see that she got it.

The rear garden of my cottage was bounded on two sides by a marshy bog and dense vegetation on the third. It was safe from prying eyes as even the closest structure was several hundred yards away. I took Dorcas by the hand and carefully guided her to the rear door of the cottage. Instinctively, I checked the back garden for anything amiss and also quickly surveyed the perimeter. *"Old habits die hard,"* I chuckled to myself.

Inside the cottage, I asked Dorcas to stay away from the windows while I lit a fire and closed the shutters. To do so, I had to go back outside through the front door and swing them inwards on their hinges, something that I did every evening at about this time. No one would suspect anything as my actions were perfectly consistent with my daily routine.

The fire was glowing warmly when I got back inside. I had intentionally not over-fed it with wood as I wanted to avoid it giving off too much light. Again, something that was consistent with my routines.

Dorcas, too, was glowing warmly. She had taken a seat on the edge of my bed with its horsehair mattress. While I watched, she removed her wimple and the combs holding her hair in place. As she shook her auburn tresses free, I was impressed by the length and shimmer in the firelight. I had always been partial to women with auburn hair, Bethany included, and even that memory could not (nor would I let it) get in the way of the moment.

I turned away from Dorcas to grab an extra quilt from the lower drawer of the highboy on the other side of the room. Turning around, I saw that she was slowly removing her outer clothing. I wanted to help, but she put a "be quiet" finger to her lips and motioned for me to to stand still. I watched as she seductively removed everything except her linen chemise and underpants – which were more like

120

men's boxer shorts than anything else. The chemise hung loosely from her shoulders but still accented the curves of her breasts and her face glowed in the firelight.

In response, I removed my own outer garments and my tunic, standing in front of her in nothing but my own linen underwear. Fortunately, I had bathed the day before and our day's net mending had focused on nets that had already dried in the sun, so they were less odiferous than usual. What happened next was entirely up to her.

Dorcas sat down on the edge of my bed. "Jonathan, please come sit next to me," she purred. I obliged and she immediately wrapped her arms around me and kissed me once again. It was even more passionate than our kiss outdoors a few minutes earlier.

"Stand up, Jonathan," she ordered in a voice that meant business.

As I stood, she grabbed the waist of my underpants and slid them off my body in one motion. Her arms came back up from my ankles and she lifted the chemise from her torso. I was now standing naked in front of a very beautiful, topless, and very horny woman.

At first, my conscience and memory of Bethany got in the way. That brief trepidation was quickly replaced by readiness as Dorcas stood, dropped her last linen undergarment to the floor and pulled me close. It was the first time I had been anywhere near a naked woman in about three years and the sight of her completely naked body made me throb with desire. I wondered just how long I would last…

Dorcas knew what she wanted and pulled me down on top of her on the bed. Spreading her legs wide, she whispered in my ear, "Jonathan, I want you to…"

Chapter Twelve: Trysts and Discoveries
New Haven, 1657 and 2018

We had spent the entire passionate night together in my bed, sleeping very little, if at all. She had not had much marital time with her previous husband, Joshua, but was a quick learner. I, of course, had plenty of experience with Bethany and other women before her – so giving Dorcas pleasure and adapting to her desires came naturally for me. I particularly enjoyed how she responded to my ministrations and stifled a loud moan of pleasure.

We explored each other's bodies completely. The scars from her whipping were fading and barely noticeable under my touch in the darkness. The scars on my hip and backside were another matter.

"Jonathan, what happened to your hip and bottom?" Dorcas asked.

I knew I could not tell her the truth and would have to invent a story. "There was an accident. A case of mistaken identity in the woodlands around Jamestown. A young Indian boy shot me with his bow and arrow, thinking I was game. The surgeon pushed the arrow through and then sewed me up. It was quite painful."

"You poor dear!" she cooed, before planting another kiss squarely on my lips and initiating another round of lovemaking.

Dorcas left my bed before dawn. She wanted to avoid any chance being seen leaving my cottage, as it would surely cause a scandal. Her home was similar to mine but located on the side of town closest to the forests and it would take her a bit of time to walk that distance. I suggested that she first walk to the harbor and take a circuitous route from there, which she did.

Strangely, though, Dorcas avoided me for the next four or five of days. I wondered if our tryst would be a one-night stand, or if it would be the foundation for something more. She finally came to me at my net mending shed and apologized for her absence.

"Jonathan, I so wanted to be with you again. Our night together showed me what I had not experienced with my late husband. If it had been up to me, we would have spent every night together since then. But… I could not control my own body, especially my monthly courses, and that is why I had to remain separate. I am so embarrassed to be telling you this, but I thought you should know."

"Dorcas, I understand exactly what you are telling me and I thank you for your honesty, even if it was embarrassing to tell me. I will tell you that there is nothing embarrassing about being a woman…"

There was a nervous pause in our conversation as we both looked away for a moment, then said almost in unison, "Tonight!" and broke out laughing.

"Yes, tonight. Once it gets dark," I told her.

"We have to be careful not to be caught," she reminded me.

*   *   *   *   *

During the day, while they were working, Bethany and Pierre were all business. Off-duty was a completely different matter. After their first tryst, they spent almost every night together in one or the other of their apartments. Bethany began to see that Pierre's arrogance in professional situations was nothing more than a cover for his social awkwardness. In fact, after that first night when he swept her off her feet, it was Bethany that was in control and dominated their relationship. Pierre, it turned out, was quite insecure and preferred not having to be creative in such situations.

The same was true for August and Sarah. They, too, had spent most of their non-working time together and rekindled their old flame. It was as if they were making up for the lost time. They were considerably older than Bethany and Pierre, but no less active or passionate in bed. In contrast to the other couple, it was August who was clearly in command. Sarah acquiesced to his whims and demands, to their mutual pleasure.

Serendipity had prevailed when Bethany leased their apartments: August and Sarah were on one floor, while she and Pierre were on another, at the opposite end of the building. There would be little chance of either couple discovering the other by accident. Bethany also trusted Maria to be discrete and not to talk about what she knew was taking place in the master bedroom.

Bethany and her team met every morning at 9 a.m. at the research site of the day. None of the other locations in New Haven had proven to be the treasure trove of information as had the old church and its cemetery, and Reverend Mather had a considerable private library of family records that went back to New Haven's earliest days.

"Mrs. Harris, I have something you might be interested in," Reverend Mather said one morning after they had been working for about a month. He was old-fashioned and always used formal terms of address. Somehow, Reverend Richard Mather had come into possession of the Captain's Log for a slaver, the *Desire*, after it docked in New Haven in 1654 to offload a cargo of slaves. "You might find it quite enlightening," he said, raising a single eyebrow for emphasis.

Pierre Delacroix had taught the team to handle any old document with extreme care, Hands were first scrubbed as if they were physicians going into the operating room, then silk gloves were donned to protect the old parchment. Documents were handled as little as possible, and then only by the edges. As each document was examined, it was left in place for the team to pore over it and make their assessments.

Bound documents, however, were much more difficult to handle. The Captain's Log was one of those documents. Reverend Mather had left it open to a specific page and weighted the verso side with a stainless-steel paperweight, careful not to put too much strain on the spine and its dried-out leather bindings. Both the paper and the bindings could disintegrate if they were manipulated too much.

Bethany was visibly nervous as she approached the viewing table. She wondered what Reverend Mather might have discovered. Quickly scanning the visible portion of the document, she was impressed by the neat handwriting and perfect spelling, neither of which were common for the date of the entry:

Captain's Private Log,

27th of August, Year of Our Lord 1654.

Added one castaway to the ship's complement, a Mister Jonathan Harris, from Jamestown in the Virginia Colony. Mister Harris was rescued from his dinghy at an approximate position of 34 degrees north, 74 degrees and 30 minutes west. This position is roughly halfway between His Majesty's Colony on Bermuda and the Carolina coast.

The small dinghy that carried Mister Harris was of a curious material. It was neither wood nor iron and when the ship's carpenter and his apprentice bored holes in the hull near the keel, It quickly filled with water but did not sink. Mister

Harris told me that it likely was possessed by demons and that we should fire on it with our weapons to break it up and send it to the deep. With my orders, we fired our various weapons and after about a quarter of an hour, the dinghy was sent to the bottom. My last memory as it disappeared was seeing "Great Escape II" on its stern.

Upon reading the last sentence, Bethany turned white as a sheet and began to wobble unsteadily on her feet. "I need to sit down, please," she said weakly.

Pierre quickly slid a chair under Bethany and guided her into a sitting position. He noticed that she was perspiring profusely and becoming more unsteady, as if she were about to faint.

"Bethany, I suggest you put your head down between you knees, or we will be picking you up off the floor," Pierre said firmly. He then went over to the table and read the log entry for himself.

'Oh, my God!" Pierre exclaimed. "August, Sarah… you must read this passage from the Captain's Log of rhe *"Desire."*

"Could it be merely a coincidence that there was a ship called the *Great Escape* back in 1654?" Sarah asked.

"It is, my dear, quite doubtful," August replied. "Ships back then generally had single-word names or were named for people of the day, usually female."

Bethany had regained her composure somewhat and joined the discussion. "Did the sailors of 1654 paint the name of their ship on the stern of tender dinghies, August? You are our maritime history expert."

"I don't believe so, Bethany," August replied. "The name was generally painted near the bow, where modern-day registration numbers would be affixed."

"Is it possible that Jonathan was somehow transported to the 17th Century?" Bethany asked, addressing the question at no one in particular.

Reverend Mather finally added his opinion. "The church frowns on me expressing this point of view, but local legends suggest that there were people back then who seemed to have come from an otherworldly place. There is no other explanation than some sort of time travel."

"I am guessing that the 'curious material' the Captain mentioned in his log was fiberglass and foam, which is what our dinghy was made of. It did, however, have a small outboard motor on the stern, which I would imagine that Jonathan jettisoned once it ran out of fuel." Her supposition could not have been more correct.

*   *   *   *   *

With Dorcas's prescribed mourning period officially over, we could establish that we were a couple. I still had feelings for Bethany, but that was another life and another century. I could not ignore what Dorcas and I shared, any more than I could forget that I was once (or was that *would be*?) married to Bethany.

Our circumstances were somewhat unusual in that we had both lost previous spouses. Dorcas's husband, Joshua, had been found dead in the woods and I had established that my wife had died in childbirth. Puritan courtship between never-married young people involved the approval of both sets of parents – which neither of us had – and the custom of "bundling," where a young couple would share a bed, albeit with a divider board between them.

Instead, we were treated as adults with familiarity of what transpires between a man and a woman in the marital bed. We were, however, warned by the minister and the deacons that they would not tolerate any inappropriate behavior between us, but stopped short of using the word "fornication."

We had to be discrete. Just like it was after our first night together, Dorcas could not tarry too long away from her home, nor could she be seen leaving mine. We were "fornicating" right under the noses of the parish elders and they were either completely unaware or turning a blind eye to our crime of passion.

As the summer wore on, Dorcas became my partner in net mending. We were never going to get rich, but we were comfortable and had everything we needed. Morning to night, our bobbins were busy repairing the damage done to the nets by a bumper harvest. We never lacked for fresh fish, as the captains always made sure we got at least one good-sized fish from each catch. Grilled striped bass tasted just as good in 1657 as they did in 2015.

When the gill net fishing slowed a little as the water warmed in Long Island Sound, it became clear to me that I should ask Dorcas to become my wife. I had given up all hope of ever returning to Bethany and the 21st Century. The need for progeny also weighed heavily on my shoulders.

I had deduced quite some time ago that a son was needed to carry on the Harris name and that it was possible I would appear twice in my own family tree: once as Jonathan Harris, husband of Dorcas, in the 1650s – and again as the husband of Bethany in the 20th Century. It was all so confusing to think about and it kept me awake many nights as I tried to make sense of it all.

Along with the troubling logic of potentially being my own ancestor, I was perplexed about being able to confide in Dorcas that I was truly an otherworldly being. Would she think I was crazy and totally off my rocker, or would she accept what I was telling her? When I wasn't thinking about the family tree issues, I was debating with myself the pros and cons of giving Dorcas more information than her limited world view could handle. In any case, I had to sell the story completely if and when I did tell her, and it certainly would not be easy.

Mulling over my own situation, I suddenly realized that I knew precious little about this woman, Dorcas Pinkerton. Heck, I didn't even know her maiden name. Where did her family come from? Was she born here in the New World? I had a laundry list of questions that needed to be answered before I could volunteer any more information about myself.

It would take time to gather information. Weeks, maybe even months, would go by before I had a complete picture of Dorcas Pinkerton. I had to treat it like a reconnaissance mission or even like I was grooming a duplicitous villager to provide me with information. Slow and steady. Gain their confidence. Build a sense of trust. They will eventually tell you everything you need to know.

It was less trouble than I had anticipated to get information from Dorcas. She already trusted me, so her providing honest answers to my questions came as naturally to her as getting out of bed in the morning. In less than a week, I knew everything there was to know about this wonderful woman.

Dorcas was twenty-two years old and was born in England in 1635. She had already told me her mother had died in childbirth, but what was more interesting was that her father brought her to the New World in 1642, aboard the *Hector,* to escape the inevitable English Civil War. Because they lived in a coastal fishing town (she could not remember the name), it was highly likely that her father, John Parham, would have been pressed into service in the Royal Navy. Her story thus far was based on her own recounting of her father's storytelling as she grew into womanhood.

The *Hector* seemed familiar to me. I remember seeing passenger manifests for several ships of the mid-17th Century, along with notations in my family tree. Could it be possible that Dorcas Parham Pinkerton crossed the Atlantic Ocean along with some of my own ancestors? Dorcas would have only been about seven years old at the time, so any memory she had of the crossing was developed through the eyes of a child. The only thing she could remember was the name of the ship and that nearly everyone aboard became violently seasick, herself included.

One afternoon, while we were mending the last nets of the day at my work shanty on the dock, a gentleman happened by who obviously knew Dorcas. A middle-aged man by appearance, he could have been about my age. I was curious about their connection.

"Dorcas Parham, it is good to see you once again," the man exclaimed in a booming basso profundo.

"Captain Tettersell… welcome home…" Dorcas replied. "I trust all is well with you?" I detected some tension in her voice, as if she was merely being polite and not exactly pleased to see the man.

"Yes, my dear, it certainly is, but only here in the New World," said Tettersell. "Back home, things are not going well for the Royalists, so I hear. The Parliamentarians have fared so well that Mister Cromwell has been offered the crown. He thankfully declined."

My curiosity was piqued, and I had to find out more. "Captain Tettersell, I am Jonathan Harris and pleased to make your acquaintance. How do you know Dorcas, now Widow Pinkerton?"

"Well, good sir, it is rather a long story," he intoned, obviously intent on launching into a saga of his life and travels to the New World. "Perhaps it is best told over a pint of New Haven's finest ale?"

"I would like that very much," I replied. I had to know more about Dorcas's background, third party source or not.

"Perhaps the lady would like to join us as well? The last time I saw her was at her father's funeral, may he rest in peace, and there is so much catching up to do." Something about the way Tettersell looked at Dorcas was quite unnerving.

We made our way to the public house that I frequented. Finding a seat in a quiet corner, I ordered pints of ale for Tettersell and myself, and a ladies' glass for Dorcas. The barmaid delivered them a few moments later, giving us a nearly toothless grin; in my time, the poor woman would have been ostracized for her lack of dental hygiene.

"Mister Harris, when Dorcas was but a wee lass, her father was a fisherman in Brighton, where I homeported my collier scow, the *Surprise*. John Parham was a gentleman above all else and a wonderful father to Dorcas."

"I see. So, you knew her father well?" I asked.

"Yes, sir. I was sad to see them leave in the Year of Our Lord Sixteen Hundred and Forty-Two, but it was for the best. John Parham was not a fighting man, and neither side in our Civil War cared whether a man had a family when they pressed him into service. Had he been killed, young Dorcas would have been left an orphan," Tettersell explained.

"How did you end up here in the Connecticut Colony, Captain?" I asked.

"Well, that's where my story gets quite interesting, you see… In 1651, after the Battle of Worcester, I was contracted by none other than King Charles II to convey him across the Channel to France. None of the crew but me knew his true identity. It was the Giffard and Pendrell families of Boscobel House and Chillington Hall who brought His Majesty to me in Brighton."

"Captain Tettersell," I interjected, "why did you not remain in England or France?"

Tettersell stroked his beard for a moment, then winked at me. "You see, Mister Harris, I am a man who understands the value of money and connection. I could not return to England under pain of death and remaining in France would not have been at all lucrative. His Majesty made it worth my while to remain abroad while leaving my beloved *Surprise* behind for his use… so here I am, no longer a merchant seaman. I am still a Captain and the owner of an ever-growing fleet of slavers making the rounds between the dark continent of Africa and the New World. I rarely go to sea these days, in favor of… shall we say… more relaxing activities ashore."

In spite of his bloviating, I found Captain Tettersell to be an interesting man. However, like most braggarts, I could take only so much of him. I decided, after that extended story of adventure, that I should remove myself from his company and invited Dorcas to do likewise. She had, after all, remained nearly silent since we sat down at the pub.

"Dorcas, may I walk you home?" I asked.

"Of course, Jonathan. I would like that very much," she replied, making sure that Tettersell heard her answer.

"Mister Harris, perhaps you will allow the lady to remain here with me for some dinner? I shall see her safely home," said Tettersell.

Dorcas gave me a look that did not need any explanation. There was fear in her eyes. She did not want to spend any more time than necessary with this man, and certainly did not wish to be left alone with him under any circumstances. I would find out soon enough what had made her so tense to be around the man.

As we left the pub, Dorcas took me by the arm and pulled me close. "Jonathan, thank you. I did not want to be left alone with *that man*. I was a newlywed when my father died and my husband, Joshua, was away tending his traplines. I was still grieving the loss of my father, but Captain Tettersell made inappropriate advances towards me just the same. The last thing I wanted at that time was to be comforted by a man that was not my husband and Captain Tettersell was not offering me the kind of 'comfort' I needed. In the end, I told him I never wanted to see him again."

"But he's here in New Haven. How do you explain that?" I asked.

"He must have heard about Joshua's demise and intended to woo me to become his wife," she answered. "I would never, under any conditions, marry Captain Tettersell… There are stories about his… well… desires… that have spread through the ladies of the town. Besides, I am already promised to you, my dear man."

"Is there anything else I should know about the man?" I asked.

"His business is located in Fairfield, and he brokers slave auctions in towns from New Amsterdam to Boston," Dorcas explained. "He has become wealthy and well-connected and can afford the finer things in life. Once people find out he is connected to the heir-apparent to the throne of England, their demeanor changes and they become quite obsequious. Personally, I find their effusiveness nauseating."

"What about the slave pens on the other side of the village green?" I asked.

"He has a controlling interest in any of the slaves that are placed there for 'fattening up,' as he says. He also owns the group of slaves that are trustees for the pens, like Fatou, the healer," Dorcas explained.

Reaching Dorcas's meager home, I took her hand in mine and gently kissed the back of it, as was customary for courting couples of the day. Public displays of affection such as kissing on the mouth were reserved for married people. As we parted, her hand lingered in mine, sending tingles of excitement up my arm – likely because I knew what was going to happen in due time once I made my way around to the rear entrance. Like Dorcas's visits to my own home, I would have to remain out of sight before reaching the back door.

*　*　*　*　*

Bethany was slowly realizing that her attraction to Dr. Pierre Delacroix was, for the time being, just lust and a need for sex, *"Really good sex,"* she mused. Their time together was blurring one moment into the next and Pierre had become smitten with JD. It had taken time, as Bethany could not sever JD from her memory of Jonathan. Once she finally unpacked that emotional baggage, allowing Pierre to take a greater role in their lives seemed natural – on the surface, at least. She still missed Jonathan terribly and hoped beyond all hope that he would someday return to them.

She was still concerned, though, by Pierre's early soliloquy where he claimed that he was happiest when he was not encumbered by a relationship. Reliving the discussion over and over again in her mind, Bethany still wasn't sure if Pierre was now sincerely interested in their strange family dynamics or if he was simply taking an "any port in a storm" approach to their relationship.

For their part, August and Sarah were officially a couple again and just as inseparable as Bethany and Pierre. Personal relationships, though, were put aside when they were at work. They had made much progress researching Jonathan's family history but were now focused on the little clues they had uncovered from Reverend Mather's holdings. There was no solid line from the Jonathan Harris of 2015 to the Jonathan Harris of the 1650s except for the manifest and Captain's Log entry from the *Desire*.

When Bethany was not with Pierre and slept alone, her dreams took her to darker times in New Haven's history. Her team had uncovered records of slave auctions, of punishments meted out by the ecclesiastical court of the day, and of general family information like baptisms, marriages, and deaths, all of which elicited dream responses during her REM sleep periods, some of them quite bizarre and morbid.

In one of her more vivid and recurring dreams, Bethany perceived the spirits of Jonathan and a faceless Dorcas Harris rising from the weathered gravestone in the church yard. Each time she had this dream, she would awaken in a cold sweat, calling out Jonathan's name. Her semi-conscious outbursts were always loud and always brought Maria running to her side.

"Why do I only have these dreams when Pierre isn't here with me?" Bethany asked out loud, addressing the question to no one in particular.

"Perhaps it is time for us to visit another psychic, Miss Bethany," Maria replied. "We are too far away from Senora Soto Contreras, but if I call her, she might be able to give us the name of a reputable seer here in Connecticut."

"Maria, I don't want to keep having these dreams. Most of all, though, I don't want to have to keep Pierre in my bed just to stop having the dreams… the nightmares."

There was a tense silence for a moment before Bethany continued, "Maria, if JD is sound asleep, will you stay here with me? It might not be just Pierre that prevents the night terrors. It could be just having the presence of another person and I need to find out."

"Of course, Miss Bethany," Maria replied as she crawled under the covers in the king-sized bed, facing away from Bethany and not quite knowing what would be an appropriate distance to keep from her employer. Bethany answered that question soon enough: she moved closer to Maria and wrapped her arms around the young woman. They both quickly fell into a blissful slumber.

The next morning, Maria awakened first and found Bethany's hand on her breast. Not quite sure what to do, she remained as motionless as possible while waiting for Bethany to wake. Maria was absolutely certain that nothing untoward had happened during the night, but now was not sure of Bethany's intentions.

Bethany began to stir, "Good morning, Maria," she whispered groggily, still in the semi-daze of slumber. "Thank you for sleeping here last night. I needed to be close to another body." Bethany unconsciously squeezed Maria's breast, suddenly realizing what she had done. "Oh... I am so sorry... that was not appropriate," Bethany said nervously.

After a short pause, Bethany spoke again. "Let me explain. When I was in the Navy, it was not unusual for women sharing a stateroom to bunk up like that when they were emotionally drained and needing comfort. Unlike doing the same thing with a man, there were no sexual overtones, and it was just the comforting that being close to another person brought. There was always inadvertent touching and we would always laugh about it."

"I understand, Miss Bethany," Maria replied, "but where I come from, a very strict and traditional home… well… It just would never have happened."

"Maria, thank you for explaining that to me. I hope you won't think badly of me… or avoid me in the future when I need…"

Maria interrupted her boss, "No, Miss Bethany, it's fine. I am a long way from home and my family – so it was nice for me, too, to be close to you."

"Then let's not say any more about it!" said Bethany. "JD should be waking up any moment."

Chapter Fourteen: First Reading
New Haven, 1657-1658

Dorcas and I had been enjoying each other's company under the cover of darkness for several months and kept each other warm through the winter. It was rather surprising that we had not been caught and punished for fornicating. Maybe it was because the people of New Haven, with its harbor area frequented by sailors, were more tolerant of such behavior. There was even a brothel just around the corner from my home and neither the constables nor the clergy paid any attention to it.

It was finally spring, and we were sitting on the workbench once again, mending the pile of nets the previous day's fishermen had left at our feet. As always, Dorcas worked more quickly and efficiently than I did. Reaching the end of her pile of nets, she turned to me and smiled.

"Jonathan, there is something I need to tell you…"

"What, pray tell, could that be?" I teased. When Dorcas started a conversation with that statement, I had learned to expect the unexpected.

She continued, "I won't be able to hide it from you much longer. I think I am with child," she beamed. "I haven't had my courses in nearly three months."

"Well, it's settled, then. We will have to get married," I said, smiling.

"Do you know about the banns, Jonathan?" she asked.

"I have been attending church right along with you and I know what they are. I will meet with Reverend MacKendrie first thing in the morning and declare our intent to marry."

Reverend MacKendrie had come over from Scotland a few years earlier and was an ordained Presbyterian minister. Free Church Presbyterianism and Puritanism seemed to go hand-in-hand and he was quickly installed as the pastor of the congregation serving the harbor area and the itinerant sailor population. A logical man of the world, MacKendrie understood the reality of life in the colonies and the way romantic relationships evolved.

"Reverend MacKendrie, I have proposed marriage to the widow Dorcas Parham Pinkerton and wish for the banns of marriage to be read, starting this Sunday or Sunday next."

MacKendrie tented his hands below his chin as if in prayer. "Of course, Mister Harris. Do you wish to marry as soon as the three readings of the banns are complete?"

"Yes, sir. That is our intent," I replied.

MacKendrie sensed some trepidation in my voice as I responded. "Is she with child, sir?"

"Yes," I replied simply.

"You know the Kirk… Church frowns on such behavior. Do you love the woman?"

"I do, with all my heart." It was the first time I had admitted my feelings to anyone. Up to this point, I had not even told Dorcas I loved her, baby on the way or not.

"Then I will read the banns as you requested, starting this Sunday. You can trust me not to reveal the true reason for your imminent marriage. Shall we pray?" MacKendrie asked.

"I would be honored for you to pray with me, Reverend." Before Dorcas, I had always questioned the existence of a higher being and had never been a praying man, not even in battle when our situation was dire. Yet here I was, asking a Presbyterian minister to pray with and for me.

Dorcas was beside herself with joy when I told her what MacKendrie had agreed to. I also told her that he had promised not to divulge her pregnancy. Though the situation was not exactly a Catholic confessional, the information was given to MacKendrie in the context of a confession. I was unsure of the religious ethics of the day, with the break from Rome having taken place just over a century earlier, but was convinced that I could trust the Reverend's discretion.

On Sunday, as promised, the service ended with the first reading of our banns:

"I publish the banns of marriage between Mister Jonathan Harris and the widow Dorcas Parham Pinkerton, both of New Haven. This is the first reading of the banns. If any of you know cause or just impediment why these two persons are not to be joined together in Holy Matrimony, you are to declare it forthwith."

Across the church, people were looking at each other as they always did when a couple announced their intentions. Women raised their eyebrows. Men pursed their lips and nodded. I looked over at Dorcas and saw her blushing as she took my hand in hers and squeezed it tightly.

As the congregation filed out of the church, we received profuse wishes of congratulations from our friends and acquaintances. Then it dawned on me: who would I have stand up for me as a witness when the blessed day came?

Dorcas was in an even worse situation. She had been ostracized by most of the village women since her public whipping two years earlier. "Jonathan, I am perplexed. I do not have anyone to stand with me at our wedding," she said as the tears began to flow.

"Reverend MacKendrie is married, I think. Perhaps we should cultivate a friendship with the Reverend and his goodwife."

"But I'm not good enough to be the friend of a minister's wife," Dorcas said dejectedly.

"Man of the cloth or not, the MacKendries are people just like you and me. We can at least try," I said, trying to reassure her.

"You always know best, my love."

A few days later, I sought out Reverend MacKendrie. "Good Reverend," I said, "would you and your goodwife dine with me and the Widow Pinkerton this evening? I cannot offer much, but I do get a daily allotment of fresh fish from the fleet. Striped bass are quite tasty and Dorcas… Widow Pinkerton… is a wonderful cook and her way of seasoning the fish is sure to be a treat."

"Mister Harris, my wife, Penelope, and I would be honored to join you for the evening meal," the Reverend replied. "At what time should be join you?"

"We are usually done mending the nets before sunset. Perhaps around 6?"

"That would be most appreciated," MacKendrie replied. "We shall bring a bottle of our finest wine to share."

It didn't surprise me that the Reverend and his wife were drinkers. "After all," the Reverend said, "our Lord and Savior, Jesus Christ, turned water into wine for people to drink." With the help of a little alcohol, I hoped they would be more relaxed and not feel like they were under the scrutiny of the entire congregation. I assured Reverend MacKendrie that it would be just the four of us for dinner and that there would be no one else partaking of our hospitality. He was, it seemed, accustomed to larger gatherings where every move he made and every word he said were being picked apart for their implications. "Pastors, and pastors' wives, can be the loneliest people in the world," Penelope MacKendrie said as we sat before the fire waiting for the last bit of dinner to cook over the spit.

It was well after midnight when the MacKendries left for their home. Both were a little tipsy, and Penelope was quite demonstrative with her intentions for the rest of the night. Meanwhile, neither Dorcas nor I thought it would be necessary for her to return home for the evening as she was already there. Dorcas, too, had something in mind other than sleep.

Chapter Fifteen: A Discovery… or Two
New Haven, April 2018

In Reverend Mather's study, Bethany and her team pored over marriage records that had been immaculately kept from about 1630 until 1950, when the municipal authorities took over the management of such records. The earliest records, up to the time of the American Revolution, also noted the reading of the banns for betrothed couples. It was August Freitag who made the breakthrough discovery.

"Look what I found," he said, excitedly. "Banns of marriage dated June of 1658. First reading on Sunday, the 16th. Betrothed: Jonathan Harris and Dorcas Parham, Widow of Joshua Pinkerton."

August's declaration stopped Bethany in her tracks. She could not believe her ears. Jonathan had remarried. "Wait… no… that was 360 years ago. I am the one he would have remarried, not Dorcas." It was all so confusing, almost like arguing if the chicken or the egg came first.

Reverend Mather quickly jumped into the conversation. "If the first reading of the banns was on June 16, the second would be on June 23 and the third and final on June 30."

"What are you saying, Reverend?" Bethany asked.

"Like I said when we started this project, people back then claimed to have had encounters with otherworldly beings, perhaps time travelers. The church has written such claims off because they largely came from uneducated and illiterate folk. I have not found a single record from any of the learned members of 1650s society like lawyers, men of the cloth, or physicians, who openly corroborated any of the rumors."

He continued, "think of it like how the local TV news gets 'eyewitness accounts.' It's usually some homeless guy, easily agitated, who claims to have seen everything that happened. Back then, it was the day laborers and housewives who tried to rationalize everything they saw or heard – and anything the slaves had to say was completely discounted as make-believe. But… and this is the big but… the more educated people could not believe that such things could actually have happened unless they had seen it with their own eyes."

"Reverend Mather, I would like to know why, whenever we are stuck on a particular piece of information, that you somehow manage to give us another piece of the puzzle,"

Pierre Delacroix asked abruptly. "It seems that you are always one step ahead of our research."

"It must be Divine Intervention. I can't explain it, but the sources just appear in the… well… I have to show you myself," Mather explained. "Would you all please follow me?"

As a group, they left the Reverend's study and went to the chancel of the church. Mather led them to a space behind the altar. After knocking three times on what appeared to be a solid wood panel, he slid it from right to left, opening a passage to a nearly vertical staircase that descended into the darkness below.

Everyone's eyes were wide with astonishment and wonder. They did not expect to see such a passage in a church that was barely large enough to accommodate a hundred worshippers. August Freitag recognized that the passage likely was modeled on the "priest's holes" in England, where outlaw Catholics would hide from government officials during the persecutions under Elizabeth I.

Reverend Mather eased himself into the confined space and carefully found the top step. As he descended and quickly disappeared from view and into the darkness, he beckoned the others to follow. Bethany was in the best physical shape of the group, followed by Pierre, and they quickly followed Mather into the abyss. There was little light to guide them on their descent.

Sarah Krankheit began complaining as she contorted her ample body to fit into the small opening. "I'm not made for this. I'm a librarian, dammit, and haven't done anything like this for at least two decades."

August Freitag, too, was grumbling as he followed Sarah. "I hope there is room enough for all of us at the bottom," he teased.

"August! Slow down. You are close to stepping on my fingers!" Sarah bellowed. "And please don't fall. You will take all of us to the bottom in one fell swoop."

August gritted his teeth to avoid making a comment that he might regret later. In their month together since the start of the project, he and Sarah had renewed the closeness they once had; it was a tenuous arrangement that could disintegrate with just one wrong word at the wrong time. They had been on eggshells with each other for the past week, neither convinced that what was happening between them was real.

As they descended the steep staircase (which was really more of a ladder than anything else), Pierre noticed subtle changes in the temperature and humidity. Above ground, it was damp, foggy, and cool – typical for the time of year. Yet, as they went underground, the temperature rose slightly and the air became very dry; he was guessing that the humidity was approaching the aridity of a desert. "That's odd..." he said aloud to no one in particular, "most caves and caverns in this area are a consistent 55 degrees Fahrenheit and somewhat damp. This one feels like the inside of a pyramid in Egypt."

"It is rather strange," Reverend Mather responded, "and I have noticed the same thing myself. What is even more unusual is that every time I come down here, new documents have replaced the ones I have taken to the surface, almost as if someone is guiding our search."

Once they all reached the bottom, with only a glow from the top of the chamber lighting their way, Reverend Mather lit a single candle. "Everyone stand still for a moment, please."

Mather took the two steps across the now-overcrowded chamber and set the candle down on a small shelf. It immediately started sputtering and flickering. Pierre cocked his head as he observed the candle's behavior.

"Reverend, the candle would not be flickering like that if there weren't some sort of air movement coming from behind it," Pierre noted.

"There's something even more interesting. Take a look at the wall next to the candle…" Mather said, pointing to the left of the candle.

"I recognize that symbol. It is a Hecate Wheel, from Greek mythology," said Pierre.

"Exactly," Mather replied. "A circle with a labyrinth inside and a spiral or some other divine symbol in the center. Some religious scholars think that the symbol for the Holy Trinity is based on a Hecate Wheel."

"The ancient Greeks believed that Hecate was connected to entrance-ways or portals, ghosts, magic, witchcraft and other things," August said, joining the discussion.

"We can debate its relevance to Greek mythology all we want, Professor Freitag, but it is certainly important to practitioners of Wicca in modern times." Pierre countered. He also sensed that a heated discussion was forthcoming between himself and Freitag and was preparing his own intellectual ammunition for the battle.

Reverend Mather also noticed the tension increasing between the two scholars. "Gentlemen, please!" Mather interjected. "We are trying to make sense of this entire situation, not debate the meaning of the Hecate Circle we see before us."

Mather continued, "There has been a church of some kind on this site since the first settlers came to New Haven. It is not surprising that it might have a connection to something otherworldly. Perhaps there was also a native Pequot burial ground or something of tribal significance nearby. Unfortunately, most of the tribe and its oral history vanished after they lost the so-called Pequot War."

Bethany had remained quiet through the entire exchange. She was mesmerised by the guttering candle near the symbolic circle and catatonically detached from the room and people around her. Nobody really noticed when she began moving towards the Hecate Circle with her arms outstretched.

Reverend Mather looked up from the discussion long enough to see Bethany about a foot away from the symbol. Her eyes were wide open, but unseeing. The closer she got to the circle, the more the candle flickered and sputtered. Reaching out, Bethany unconsciously traced the entire 360 degrees of the outer circle counterclockwise with the forefinger of her right hand. Still aware of neither time nor place, both forefingers moved to the unending labyrinth, tracing each layer slowly and purposefully.

Suddenly, her eyes widened and her hands were drawn to the center symbol. Placing her left palm over the symbol and her right hand over her left, it was as if a strong magnet were pulling her into the symbol itself. Frozen there for a few seconds, the candle spluttered, then went out – as if one of the others in the tiny room had extinguished it with a breath.

Sarah Krankheit nearly panicked in the darkness and stifled a scream just as Pierre, the ever-prepared Pierre, pulled a small flashlight from his pocket. The small light seemed to calm Sarah, albeit only temporarily.

"You've had that there all along?" August scolded.

"Yes, but… with the good Reverend's guidance and storytelling, I certainly did not want to spoil the moment," Delacroix responded.

As Pierre shined his flashlight around the room, they all noticed something peculiar: Bethany Harris was gone. It was as if she had vanished into thin air. That realization brought a blood-curdling scream from Sarah and a cold sweat from the corpulent body of August Freitag.

"She couldn't have just vanished," Reverend Mather said, his voice unconvincing.

"August, did she pass you on the stairway?" Pierre asked.

"There was no way she could have gotten past me," August responded. "It's a very small space and I am a very large man."

"Like Thomas the Apostle, my mind does not believe what my eyes have seen," Reverend Mather mumbled, barely loud enough for the rest of them to hear.

Mather approached the Hecate Circle, but did not feel compelled to touch it, nor to trace its patterns. It was as if he were staring at an inanimate rock on a cold winter morning. Nothing. No sense of anyone or anything nearby. There was no magnetic pull towards the symbol like there was with Bethany. He wondered if the candle might have something to do with it, so he re-lit it. Its flame remained stable and steady with no flickering nor spluttering. In other words, normal.

"Don't you think it is odd that the candle is burning as a stable flame right now," Pierre asked.

"Whatever was causing the flickering earlier is gone," Mather observed. "I have no idea what it could have been."

"I still don't understand what's happened. Bethany was here one minute, then gone the next," Sarah added.

August summed up the situation perfectly: "The simple truth is that Bethany has vanished."

Chapter Sixteen: Strange Feelings
Connecticut, 1658

"Where am I?"

"How did I get here?"

"Where's JD? Is he safe?"

Bethany's mind was racing as the awareness of her surroundings returned. She certainly wasn't in that godawful "priest's hole" under the church altar – but where exactly was she? Moving her hands down her own body from head to toe, she suddenly realized that she was completely naked. Naked and cold. Naked, cold, and away from JD. Naked, cold, away from JD and Pierre. *"Pierre? How did he take over my thoughts? He doesn't belong here..."* She felt a panic attack coming on as her mind raced. *"I mustn't panic..."* she repeated to herself over and over.

Eventually regaining her composure, thanks largely to her military training, Bethany saw that she was in a wooded area with no signs of civilization anywhere nearby. The only sounds to be heard were those of birds chirping merrily in the trees. She tried to concentrate and hear more of civilization – like cars, automobiles, or airplanes. Nothing.

The one thing that suggested any sort of human life nearby was a smell. It was more of an aroma wafting on the breeze. It suggested roasting meat of some kind but was not like any other cook-out smells Bethany had ever encountered.

Her survival training in the Navy had taught her that shelter and water were the two most important things for sustaining life. Right now, she had neither and finding a way to stay warm was of paramount importance. *"Finding shelter and clothes, too, would be nice,"* she thought to herself.

Suddenly, the birds exploded into flight. Something – or someone – had spooked them. In the middle of a blowdown surrounded by broad-leafed vegetation, she was safe from prying eyes if it was a "someone," but not entirely safe from a "something" like a bear or a wolf.

Peeking through the leaves, she saw a young woman in Native American attire. Bethany could not help but notice how beautiful the young woman was, almost like the cartoon representations of Pocahontas in Virginia. Bethany wondered if the woman was armed and could see only a knife, sheathed on the woman's waist belt.

Standing up, but still modestly covered by the vegetation, Bethany revealed her presence. The movement in the bushes startled the young woman. Taking a defensive posture, the Indian maiden quickly drew her knife from its sheath. It happened so fast that Bethany wasn't sure she had even seen the movement.

Standing absolutely motionless, Bethany made eye contact with the woman while maintaining her modesty. "Do you speak English?" Bethany asked.

"Yes, mistress, I do. I was taught by the Reverend Eaton when I was a child."

"What is your name?"

"They call me *Aiyana*. It means 'eternal bloom' in the language of my people."

"Aiyana, you can call me Bethany. It is in the Bible."

"Yes, I know. It is from the story of Lazarus."

"So, you are a Christian?"

"Yes, Bethany. I was baptized as a baby, eighteen summers ago, when the first English came to this area."

"Aiyana, I need you to help me. I found myself here, naked, and have no idea how I got here. Could you please fetch me some clothing or a blanket? I am also very thirsty."

"Of course, Bethany. My village is not far. If I run like a deer, I will be back very soon. For now, you can have my water carrier."

Aiyana reached carefully over the bush and handed Bethany the water carrier, made from a goat's stomach. She knew that white women were more modest than the women of her tribe, which explained Bethany's hiding in the bush. White women covered themselves in all situations. Aiyana smiled at how ridiculous this was: when she was working in the fields tending their crops with her mother, they put comfort ahead of modesty. It was not unusual for all of the women of a village to be working together, undressed down to the waist. Not dwelling on the cultural differences any longer, Aiyana was, as she put it, off like a deer.

While Aiyana was gone, Bethany had time to think and recount the memory of what had happened before... before she ended up wherever and whenever this was. Bethany remembered the intensity of the night before, with Pierre, and blushed. She remembered the old church, Reverend

Mather, and climbing down a ladder of some sort under the altar, but nothing after she reached the bottom of that ladder. It was as if her mind had been erased and there was a gap until she found herself here in the woods, apparently far from any *modern* civilization.

As she looked around, Bethany noticed a very large oak tree about fifty feet away. Carved on the oak was an elaborate circle with a labyrinth shape inside. "I've seen that icon somewhere before…" she said out loud, "but where? I will have to ask Aiyana about it when she returns."

*   *   *   *   *

Dorcas and I were busy mending the nets from the fleet's outing of the day before. We worked almost nonstop, but still managed to make eye contact with each other and smile. Conversation was unnecessary.

With the first reading of our banns having taken place in church the previous Sunday, we could be a little more open with our affection for each other. Everyone now knew that we were a betrothed couple – but they did not know about Dorcas's "delicate condition," as she had not yet started to show.

Around noon, just before our midday meal break, I sensed something that I could not identify. It was like someone was dropping ice chips down my back at regular intervals, making me shudder. Dorcas noticed my unease.

"Jonathan, you seem distracted today," Dorcas commented just as we were getting ready to stop work for our mid-day meal.

"I don't know what it is, my darling. It's as if someone is standing behind me. A presence, if you will," I replied. The first image that came to my mind was from a series of sci-fi movies, my favorites, where the spiritual presence of others permeated everything.

"There certainly is not!" Dorcas exclaimed. "If someone were standing behind you, I would certainly see them. Maybe you've been visited by one of those ghosts you warned Captain Palmer about when he rescued you?" Dorcas chided, stifling a playful giggle.

"It's as real as it can be, Dorcas. Don't… mock… me." I shocked myself with the sternness of my reply and instantly regretted my tone. I was going to be in big trouble.

"Jonathan Harris! I will not have you talking to me that way. I am your betrothed, not some fishwife or harpy. It is good for a man and almost-wife to share a little silliness now and again, and that was my only intent. I wanted to lighten the dark mood you are in today." I saw tears welling up in her eyes as she spoke, something that was happening more and more lately. I was pretty certain her moodiness was related to the pregnancy.

I had to get myself out of the situation. "Dorcas, my darling, I am so sorry. Something has come over me today and I am not sure what it is. Maybe we should stop working for our meal and come back to this with our bellies full. We can go to the public house if you wish." It was the best I could do to defuse the situation and calm her down. At first, she sullenly stood her ground but eventually acquiesced to my suggestion of a nice meal away from the wharf.

During the meal, our conversation was forced and more inane small talk than usual. Perhaps it was because we were at the public house and not in a more private setting. We both noticed the tension between us, but neither of us had anything to offer in the way of easing it.

"I fear it will be stormy tomorrow," I offered. Talking about the weather usually distracted Dorcas from whatever it was that was making her angry.

"It looks that way. The wind has changed and blows warm from the west," Dorcas replied.

"Perhaps the storms will keep the fishermen at home, and we can enjoy a day of rest?" Dorcas didn't miss a thing; she fully understood what I had in mind.

"Once again, Jonathan Harris, you are preoccupied with filling every available moment with things that we should not be doing until after we are married. Mind you, I enjoy it as much as you do, but we are being watched by the deacons for any signs of impropriety." Dorcas was once again lecturing me on the virtue of temporary abstinence, important during daylight hours. "You can certainly wait a little more than another fortnight."

I bit my tongue to keep from replying inappropriately. I knew she was right, but on the other hand, we had already opened that door and there was no return from crossing that threshold, legally married or not. We were, after all, in 20th Century parlance, consenting adults. Besides, she was already pregnant, another thing from which we could not turn back.

Even distracted by Dorcas's beauty, I still felt that something was "off." Try as I might, I could not put my finger on it. It was as if I was at a séance and trying to figure out the theatrics of the so-called medium. I had to find out what was behind the sensations. I wanted answers. I was used to getting the answers I needed by whatever means necessary, legal or otherwise.

*   *   *   *   *

Back in the woods, Aiyana had finally returned to Bethany's location. She had a bundle of something strapped to her back.

"Bethany? Where are you?" Aiyana said cheerfully.

"Over here. In the bushes," Bethany responded, "I am so cold." Her teeth were chattering so loudly that Aiyana could hear the sound from several feet away. Bethany was curled up in a near fetal position to conserve body heat, making it difficult for Aiyana to find her at first.

"I have clothes for you and a blanket, but first we must warm you up as my grandmother taught me," Aiyana said. "Please step out into the clearing."

Bethany did as she was told, nakedness be damned. She was nearing the point of hypothermia and moved like a zombie. She could only stare as Aiyana laid out a bearskin rug, removed her own clothes, and then wrapped them both in a warm bearskin robe. Even in her lethargic state,

Bethany noticed how beautifully proportioned Aiyana was, and it was obvious that she had not yet borne children.

Wrapped together naked under the bearskin robe, Aiyana pulled Bethany close, face to face and torso to torso. The heat exuded by Aiyana's young lithesome body quickly warmed Bethany; she cuddled closer and began falling asleep.

"You sleep, Bethany. I will be here with you until you are ready to come with me to our village," Aiyana whispered soothingly as she stroked Bethany's hair, but Bethany had not heard a word. She was already fast asleep.

Bethany hallucinated as she slept. One minute, she was seeing Pierre, Reverend Mather, August, and Sarah; the next, it was Jonathan, JD and Maria. She dreamed that JD was calling out to her, but he was across a raging river that she could not cross.

Eventually, the dreams all blended together, with Senora Isabella Ava Soto Contreras waving her hands over them as if she were a puppeteer controlling marionettes. Bethany grunted and groaned in her sleep, then awoke with a blood-curdling scream. She clutched Aiyana tightly for comfort.

"Bethany, you had a bad dream. My people believe that such dreams are signs of the spirit world trying to contact you," Aiyana said as she stroked Bethany's hair like a mother would do with a frightened child.

"Where am I?" Bethany asked.

"You are in Quinnipiac territory, near what the English call 'Newhaven,'" Aiyana answered. Bethany noticed that Aiyana said the town's name as if it were a single word.

"How did I get here?" Bethany was puzzled.

"That is a mystery that only our spirit guide will solve," Aiyana explained. "There have been others – "

"What do you mean by 'others', Aiyana?" Bethany interrupted.

"It is forbidden for us to speak of these people without our spirit guide, my grandmother. If she allows it, you will be told," Aiyana replied. "Come, get dressed. It is time for us to go. You are hungry and food is ready."

"I can smell it roasting on the fire," Bethany noted as she began to salivate. She realized that she had not had anything substantial to eat since early that morning, whenever *that* was. "I am curious as to what manner of meat I am smelling."

It was the first time Bethany had ever been exposed to the natural feel of deerskin against her flesh and she needed Aiyana's help to don the garments. The top was quite form-fitting – except in the chest, of course – but one of the most comfortable garments Bethany had ever worn. It instantly made her warm.

Aiyana brought the conversation back to the food. "I think your people call it 'venison,' the meat of a deer," Aiyana answered. "Let's be on our way."

*　*　*　*　*

After we finished our mid-day meal, Dorcas and I were walking back to the wharf. Because we were now considered a couple, it was appropriate for her to take my left arm with her own right hand. It was my understanding that the woman-on-the-man's-left position was so that the man could, if necessary, draw a weapon to protect the woman.

Passing an empty bench outside one of the shops, Dorcas asked me to sit with her for a moment. There was no one else around, as the retail shops all closed at approximately the same time for their mid-day meal. The street was eerily silent as we sat.

"Jonathan, I need to know…" Dorcas said, taking both of my hands in hers.

"What is it, my darling?" I replied.

She looked me in the eye and squeezed my hands firmly. "Do you wish for a son or a daughter?"

"As long as you and the baby are both healthy after the birth, it does not matter to me which it might be," I replied.

"So, you are not worried if it is a daughter and unable to carry on your family name?"

"It is not of concern," I said. "A daughter will still be a Harris, even when she has grown up and gotten married. No man nor a change of name can take that away from her."

"But my first husband only wanted boys. He was firm in his belief that they were needed to work and to carry on the family name. I shudder to think what would have happened if we had been blessed with a daughter… He was not the kindest man. A good provider, yes, but as mean and ornery as a mule."

"I promise you that I will be neither mean nor ornery, Dorcas. I am just not that way," I said, leaning forward to kiss her gently on the forehead. "Once we are married, you will see!"

"I didn't think so, but it has kept me worried at night, mostly when we are apart." The tears which she had just brought under control started again.

Chapter Seventeen: In the Indian Village
Connecticut, 1658

As they approached the village, Bethany's hunger kicked into high gear. She would have eaten just about anything, but, as Aiyana had said a few moments earlier, it was venison roasting on hot rocks next to the communal cooking fire. Bethany could also see what looked like potatoes roasting on green sticks propped over the fire.

The social order of the Quinnipiac village was well-established. Before Bethany would be allowed to eat as a guest, it was Aiyana's duty to introduce Bethany to her mother and grandmother. Like most other Native American tribes, the dwindling Quinnipiacs were a matriarchal society, with grandmothers revered above all other women. The oldest grandmother in the village was the decision-maker for when they would move, who would marry whom, and what interaction the people would have with outsiders, especially the English.

Aiyana's grandmother, *Chepi*, was the oldest of the grandmothers and as such, she was considered their sachem. "Chepi," Aiyana explained, "means 'ghost', which is proper for her as she is also our spirit guide."

Bethany was taking it all in. She had not paid much attention to the history of Native Americans in either high school or college – other than the Westerns of her youth and their portrayal of most Native Americans… Indians… as "the enemy." It was an awakening for her to realize that the Quinnipiac social order was well-established and quite civilized. She wanted to learn more.

The roasted venison and potatoes were cooked to perfection; Bethany was hooked. She thought that venison was substantially better than the beef she had eaten in her other life, before the jump 360 years backwards in time. She also wondered what other culinary delights her hosts would provide in the coming days. Until she could figure out what had happened to transport her back to pre-industrial Connecticut, Bethany made up her mind that she would be the model guest.

For the next week, Aiyana did her best to immerse Bethany in Quinnipiac culture, even going so far as to teach some of the "womanly" skills like hide tanning and cooking over an open fire. At first, treating the hides turned Bethany's stomach. The traditional method used the brains of the dead animal and rendered bear fat, both of which were quite pungent. Cooking over an open fire, however,

180

made Bethany hungry – especially after her first exposure to roasted venison. The delectable smells overrode the nauseating pungency of the tanning process.

"Aiyana, would it be possible for you to take me to Newhaven so I can see how the English settlers live?" Bethany asked after she had been in the village for about two weeks.

"We will have to ask my grandmother," Aiyana replied. "It is her decision if it is wise to allow you such a visit."

Still trying to be the model guest, Bethany's reply was conciliatory. "Yes, of course. We will do what Chepi allows us to do." Inside, Bethany was anxious to be among her own English-speaking kind once again. The gap of 360 years didn't matter to her at all. She had enjoyed her time with Aiyana's people, but always having to rely on a translator was becoming tedious.

With Aiyana translating, Bethany pleaded with Chepi, "Grandmother Chepi, I would like to visit the English. I am thankful for your hospitality here in your village and I could make this my home, but I am English and should return to my own kind."

Chepi was silent for several moments. She appeared to be deep in thought. Her eyes were closed and her head bowed as if she was in prayer. Eventually, she spoke.

"Shivering One, it is right for you to want to be with your own people. We, too, would like you to stay among us. If you wish, Aiyana may take you to their village tomorrow morning."

Bethany could not contain her excitement and she broke with protocol, pulling Chepi close in a firm hug. "Thank you, Grandmother Chepi! Thank you a thousand times over." Chepi tensed at the unusual display of affection.

Turning to Aiyana, Bethany began a rapid-fire series of questions. "What time will we be leaving? How do we get there? Do I need to carry a knife? How will the English treat us?"

"Bethany, please try to sit quietly for a few moments and take in what my grandmother has told you," Aiyana said firmly. "It is most unusual for us to allow anyone of our tribe to mingle with the whites, mostly to protect our women. More than once, drunken white men have been improper. Women of my age, without husbands, have to be careful."

"I understand, Aiyana," Bethany replied.

"We shall be ready to leave just after our morning meal," Aiyana explained. "It will take us about two hours to walk there. The place of their fishing boats is the closest to us and our people routinely go there to trade for fish. It is far easier for that than it is for us to catch our own."

"Easier? How?" Bethany asked.

"The settlers have boats that can go much further from shore than our canoes and longboats, and they use nets to catch the fish. It is not our way." Bethany noticed a contemptuous tone in Aiyana's description.

Aiyana continued, "Still, our men trade crops and game for the fish – and sometimes for knives or other tools, even guns."

"I can't wait to see how the English live," Bethany said, ending the conversation for the time being.

Chapter Eighteen: A Visit to the English Settlement
Newhaven, 1658

During the walk to Newhaven, Bethany and Aiyana talked almost constantly. Bethany's curiosity and Aiyana's willingness to share her insights on Quinnipiac life made for an interesting journey. They talked of men, of love, of family – but only in general terms. Aiyana avoided asking Bethany any questions about where she had come from or what it was like there.

"Do your people marry for love?" Bethany asked Aiyana. "You are so beautiful that any man would be proud to have you for a wife, even if he didn't really love you."

"We marry when the time is right and both families agree. But…. We can bring an end to being married simply by asking Grandmother Chepi for permission. If she agrees, the man moves out and the woman is allowed to take a new husband when she is ready. It does not happen very often, as we are proud of our families staying together."

"I was married before I came here. He was a good man, but he disappeared when we were on an ocean voyage. I do not know what happened to him," Bethany explained.

"Perhaps you will find a new husband someday," Aiyana noted. "It might even be one of the Quinnipiac men. One cannot help with whom they fall in love."

"Don't you want to keep your bloodlines separate from the English?" Bethany was puzzled, as she had assumed that the intermingling of cultures was frowned upon.

"It is only the Puritans that want to keep us apart. We understand what love means, even if it is with an English person."

"So, it is okay for Quinnipiac women to marry white men?"

"In our eyes, yes," Aiyana replied.

"What happens if a woman cannot give her man children?"

"That is one of the reasons Chepi will allow them to separate as man and wife. If twelve moons... your months... have gone by and the woman is not with child, it is her choice if she wants to stay married."

"My husband and I were married for many years..." Bethany stopped short of revealing that she had had a child later in life.

"Were there no children?" Aiyana asked.

"I would like not to talk about it," Bethany replied, her tone less than cordial. Aiyana was visibly disappointed; in her culture, such things were always shared with other women, often in gory and excruciating detail. Such talk was never suitable for men; it was always "women's business."

To be sure that the Puritan constables did not see Bethany as a white woman, in addition to her buckskin attire, she had been disguised with a Quinnipiac headband and her face rubbed with red clay to give her skin a more native tone. When the two women reached the first constabulary outpost about a half mile from the fishing fleet's docks, they passed through without question. It was common to see Quinnipiac women coming and going from the primitive fish market, so Bethany and Aiyana were nothing out of the ordinary in the eyes of the less-than-attentive constables.

Bethany wrinkled her nose and nearly gagged at the smell of decaying piscine offal. The tide was out when the day's catch was unloaded and cleaned, so the detritus on the mudflats was fully exposed to the sun. Aiyana, on the other hand, didn't seem the least bit affected by the smell.

"It must be all that hide tanning using brains and blood," Bethany thought to herself.

A short way away, under the overhang of a small shed, Bethany could see a man and a woman busily at work repairing a pile of fishing nets.

"There's something familiar about the man working on the nets. I recognize his movements and the shape of his head…" Bethany said in a voice just above a whisper.

"Do you want to get closer, Bethany?" Aiyana asked. "He might know something about your past if he is indeed someone you know."

"I'd rather just wait here and watch for a few minutes. I am sure it will come to me," Bethany replied.

Near where Bethany was attempting to conceal herself, a broadsheet had been posted on the side of a building. It was fairly fresh; the ink had not run from being exposed to moisture and the paper was entirely intact. Across the top of the sheet was a date: "June 24, in the Year of Our Lord 1658."

"*Sixteen fifty-eight?*" Bethany whispered to herself. "*You've got to be fucking kidding me.*" Had anyone been within earshot of her salty language, she would have been pilloried – or worse.

Bethany turned back to the waterfront, hoping that the broadsheet was just a dream. When she turned back, it was still there. It was real. She could touch it. It fit with the surroundings.

Taking a deep breath to compose herself, Bethany turned back to the waterfront. So far, the couple at the nets did not seem to be aware that they were being watched. They continued about their work, talking quietly to each other; it was obvious from their mannerisms and occasional physical contact that they were a romantically involved couple. Bethany was still trying to figure out how the man was familiar.

*   *   *   *   *

When I was in hostile environments in places I still can't talk about, I always developed a sixth sense as my familiarity with the surroundings increased. I *knew* when something was amiss. I *knew* when trouble was nearby. The sensations always evoked a very strong and defensive fight-or-flight response.

Not wanting to alarm Dorcas, I nonchalantly stood up, pecked her on the forehead, and told her I was going to the privy. She did not notice that I had slipped my net knife up the sleeve of my tunic. If a weapon was necessary, I would not be afraid to use it. Hand-to-hand combat with knives was something at which I had excelled in my military days.

I slowly strolled from my net mender's shanty to the nearest privy. My head was on a swivel the entire time, looking for things that might seem out of place and potential ambush threats. The only thing I saw was two Native women engaged in a conversation near the place where the fishermen dumped their offal. I used my peripheral vision to keep them in sight as best I could without making it obvious that I was watching them.

It didn't seem unusual, but as I observed their limited conversation, it became obvious that one of the women was extremely nervous. She fidgeted more than a normal Native woman would have. Her eyes darted from point to point like a cornered animal looking for an escape route. I sensed that she knew I was watching her, but she avoided making eye contact.

Eventually, she turned away from me as the women prepared to leave. I couldn't place it, but I had seen the woman before. I never forgot a shapely backside, and hers certainly was one of the shapeliest I had ever seen, Native woman or not. *"Wait a minute, Jonathan... you're getting married soon,"* I told myself, *"you can't be drooling over other women like that!"* Despite my self-admonition, I knew I had to see that woman again.

When I got back to the nets and Dorcas, she could sense that something was on my mind. I decided to remain taciturn for the time being, as it was nothing concrete yet, just a premonition or maybe another case of *déjà vu* like I had experienced earlier in my time on the New Haven waterfront. Who was that woman? Was she really white and only disguised as a Native? She certainly didn't move with the confidence of a Quinnipiac woman...

*   *   *   *   *

Aiyana and Bethany headed back to the Quinnipiac village. Bethany was deep in thought the entire time and hardly spoke. *"He certainly looked like Jonathan and even moved like Jonathan,"* she mused to herself. *"But it can't be... he's been declared dead."* Her thoughts kept spinning out of control. *"The people in that old church probably think I am dead, too, yet here I am..."*

Back in the Quinnipiac village, Bethany was suddenly exhausted. The combination of the walk to Newhaven and the feeling that she was seeing Jonathan – or one of his ancestors – weighed heavily. All she wanted to do was to lie down and take a nap. It was nearing sunset, so it wouldn't be long until mealtime and the evening's activities around the fires would make it impossible to sleep before Chepi bade everyone good night and quiet was restored.

Heading to the hut that she and Aiyana now shared, Bethany curled up on the bearskin rug and pulled a well-tanned robe over her body for warmth. Aiyana came in just as Bethany was falling asleep.

"Bethany, you will be on your own for a few days," Aiyana said as she was gathering her extra bearskin robe and a change of clothing. "It is my time to bleed and it is our custom that I live apart until it passes."

"Is there anyone else in the village who speaks English as well as you do? I do not want to be without someone to translate," Bethany pleaded.

"Yes, there is one man who was taught by Reverend Eaton. He, too, was baptized as a Christian. His name is *Nechochwen.* It means 'he who walks alone.' Nechochwen has never taken a wife, and he might be a good match for you. Chepi gave him that name because he did not seem to

192

be interested in a wife." Aiyana beamed with pride as a potential matchmaker and ending Nechochwen's celibacy.

Aiyana continued, "I will have Grandmother Chepi introduce you to him at the evening fire. I cannot because… well… I already told you."

Bethany was no longer tired. Her sleepiness had been replaced by a bad case of first-meeting jitters – something she hadn't experienced since she was introduced to Jonathan two decades before they retired from the Navy, *"Who was this Nechochwen and why did Aiyana think he was a good match, a potential husband?"* she thought as Aiyana walked away.

There was also the unresolved issue of the man at the net mender's hut on the waterfront. He certainly bore a resemblance to Jonathan. That alone made Bethany weak at the knees. She knew she had to be careful not to give Nechochwen the wrong impression, that she might be interested, until she had figured out why the netminders intrigued her the way he did. There was one fact that stuck with her from the research she had been doing in the 21st Century: one Jonathan Harris died in July 1658 and would be buried in the church yard where she had seen the tombstone.

After the evening meal, Chepi introduced Bethany to Nechochwen. He was a total gentleman and thoroughly fluent in English. Reverend Eaton had taught him well. Bethany was immediately impressed with Nechochwen's intellect, conversational skills, *and* his good looks. It was a warm evening and, as was customary, the men of the village were shirtless, dressed only in buckskin trousers and a loincloth. Bethany remembered Pierre Delacroix for a comparison; Nechochwen's muscled physique put Pierre to shame. She needed to be cautious that her own lust did not override her good judgment.

Nechochwen was a model host for the evening. He made Bethany laugh on more than one occasion and the looks they were getting from the elders, and Chepi especially, were approving. If she couldn't resolve the Jonathan look-alike issue within the week, she thought that she could easily find herself in Nechochwen's arms.

Chapter Nineteen: In Camp
In the Quinnipiac Village, 1658

Bethany found it rather odd that she had been paired with Nechochwen, a much-younger man. He was slightly older than Aiyana, in his early twenties. Bethany, on the other hand, was in her late forties.

After the evening meal, around the fire, Bethany dared ask how old Grandmother Chepi was. With Nechochwen translating, Chepi said that she had seen fifty-five harvests. Chepi's appearance, by 21st Century comparisons, was more like that of an eighty-year-old. Her skin was wrinkled and leathery, her hair the texture of straw, some of her teeth were missing (what few remained were badly decayed), and her left eye was clouded by a nearly opaque cataract.

"I have lived longer than nearly all of the Quinnipiac women ever have," Chepi explained. "only my own grandmother, who we all knew as 'the old one,' lived longer. She went to the spirit world after sixty-five harvests."

Through Nechochwen, Chepi asked Bethany, "How many harvests have you seen, my visiting granddaughter?"

"Grandmother Chepi, I have seen forty-eight harvests," Bethany replied sheepishly.

"You look no more than thirty harvests," Chepi said, pursing her lips for emphasis. "Have you spent your entire life in a lodge, out of the sun, the rain, and the cold?"

"No, I have not," Bethany responded, pausing to gather her thoughts for the rest of her response. "Where I come from, the women are equal to the men, and we provide the same labor for our survival."

Chepi's next line of questions was much more personal. "Have you had a husband? Children? Can you still bear children?"

Nechochwen was obviously embarrassed by what he was having to translate; such talk was normally reserved for the 'women's lodge" where Aiyana was now resting. He wished Aiyana were there. He knew the words, but it made him uncomfortable to be the intermediary between the two women.

Bethany answered the older woman's questions in the order they were presented. "I had a husband, but he was lost at sea. It was many years ago." Bethany knew that precision in her answers would just bring more questions.

"Grandmother Chepi, with respect, I do not wish to talk about being a mother or being able to be one. It is too distressing and too personal for me." Bethany hoped that this approach would put an end to Chepi's questions. She might have stymied the discussion of motherhood, but JD was foremost in her thoughts. *"Was he okay? Was he still making progress on his toilet training? Was Maria making sure he was fed and bathed?"*

"I understand," Chepi replied as she nodded, then turned to stare into the fire.

Nechochwen was confused. The visitor was worthy of being his wife, but so much older than he was. Would she be able to be a wife to him in every sense of the word, to come to him in the night, to lie together? Could she give him a son? It was not unusual for older Quinnipiac men to take younger wives, but it was highly unusual for a much older woman to take such a young man for a husband. He had to admit that he found the white woman quite attractive, despite her advanced age. She certainly did not look like a woman of forty-eight harvests!

As the adults around the fire retired to their huts to sleep or perhaps copulate, Nechochwen escorted Bethany back to the hut she shared with Aiyana. They remained a respectful distance apart and said little. Before going inside, she turned to face him.

"Nechochwen, thank you for translating for me tonight and for seeing me safely back to my hut. I know what you are thinking, that I might be too old for you to consider as a wife, but please know that I will make my decision in due time. With Grandmother Chepi's permission, of course."

She felt it was the appropriate time to explain to him that it was unlikely she could give him children. "I must tell you that I probably can no longer bear children, Nechochwen. If you must become a father, I ask that you look to another."

Nechochwen looked away briefly when he heard Bethany's statement about children. The silence was tense for a moment before he spoke, seeming to dismiss her comment. "Nothing will happen without the Grandmother's permission," he replied. Bethany noticed the odd use of the definite article before Chepi's title of "Grandmother." It was not the first time she had heard the usage in English translations from the Quinnipiac tongue.

"I would like to go back to the fishing wharf tomorrow," Bethany said calmly, "and I would like you to escort me."

"The English have seen me before and know I am without a wife. Some of them think I prefer the company of men…" His downcast gaze spoke of extreme embarrassment by the accusations. "With you by my side, Bethany, they will not think that any longer," he explained.

Bethany had to stifle a giggle. The white men of Newhaven thought Nechochwen was gay! She would just have to prove them wrong.

"Good night, Nechochwen."

"Good night, Bethany."

A little after midnight, Bethany woke suddenly. She had heard a child calling out, thinking it was JD. *"I have to focus on my own survival here – or I won't ever get back to JD,"* she repeated over and over, as if it had become her new mantra, eventually returning to sleep.

* * * * *

The dawn was one of the most glorious Bethany had seen since her mysterious arrival ten days earlier. The rising sun reflected off the low clouds in hues of red, orange and gold. The air was crisp and calm. Birds were singing in the trees, to be silenced only as the village came out of its slumber. The setting, she observed, was almost idyllic. It reminded her of life aboard ship, as the night watch was relieved and the day departments began their routine – minus the hum of the ship's machinery, of course.

After visiting the women's toilet area in the woods, Bethany joined the adult women to assist with preparing breakfast. With the smell of cooking food, the men began rousing from their huts as well. Mornings, Bethany noticed, were more about routine than anything else; Aiyana had already explained how the village traditions governed everyday life.

Bethany was assigned the job of stirring the porridge, which was cooking in a large iron cauldron suspended from a tripod. She wondered where they had gotten the cauldron and would ask Nechochwen to translate her question as soon as he arrived from the men's toilet area. She guessed that it had been acquired in a trade shortly after the Puritans' arrival.

The women hummed and sang softly as they prepared the morning meal. Occasionally, there was a primitive harmony. Bethany felt like she belonged here in some ways, but an intruder in others. She was still mystified by her sudden appearance in this particular setting, which she had learned was exactly 360 years before her own time.

If she couldn't find a way back to her own time, Bethany was prepared to assimilate into the Quinnipiac culture and adopt these people as her own, learning their language and customs. Their lives were so much simpler than the hustle and bustle of the 21st Century. The matriarchal social order was all about age and seniority, not about who could climb over someone else to get ahead. The simplicity of it all was something that Bethany had wanted in her own life once JD was born.

Sure, she had Maria as an *au pair* which brought a degree of simplicity. But… there were play dates and preschool, potty training and new foods, "big boy beds" and cribs. All of them were added complications to what should have been a simpler life, a symbiotic relationship between mother, child, and her helpers – which, in Quinnipiac culture were the adolescent girls still a little too young to take husbands but old enough to learn how to be a wife and mother. *"I wish JD were here with me to share this experience,"* she mused.

After the men had all eaten and left for a day of fishing, the women and children ate their morning meal. It was a boisterous affair, with all shapes and sizes of children scurrying around. Regardless of who their biological mother might have been, it took one word from the any of the mothers – or even the teenage girls – to stop any misbehavior in its tracks. Bethany was amazed by the respect the children showed their elders, unlike what she had seen in her own time.

Bethany noticed that Nechochwen had not gone fishing with the other men. Instead, he appeared to be waiting for her to finish her chores so he could escort her to Newhaven and the fishing wharf as she had requested and he had promised. He was sitting on the ground, leaning back against a large tree trunk, watching her every move. She was more than a little bit embarrassed by his attention.

The children dispersed to play and the women quickly cleaned up the remains of the morning meal. As Bethany worked, she kept giving Nechochwen furtive glances. It was hard to avoid eye contact as he was constantly looking in her direction.

When Bethany's work was done, she called out, "Nechochwen, I am ready for you to take me to town now."

Chapter Twenty: In Newhaven Again
June 1658

With Nechochwen at her side, Bethany was once again dressed to hide the fact that she was a white woman. They covered the distance to the fishing wharf in much less time than she and Aiyana had done about a week earlier, in part because Nechochwen did not engage in idle conversation.

"Men," he told Bethany, "talk only when necessary, and when they do, it is about important things like hunting and fishing. Not about children or having children, except with their wife. Everything else is women's talk."

Once again, Bethany had to stifle a chuckle. Nechochwen had no idea what lay ahead for men in general nor that traditional gender roles would begin breaking down in about three hundred years. He would be surprised to learn that in some occupations, the military in particular, it was normal for women to be in charge and not subservient to men. "That,' she thought to herself, "was a discussion for another time."

Her main goal in Newhaven was to get closer to the net mender and his female companion. Based on her recollection of a headstone not long before she mysteriously appeared in 1658, the man could be Jonathan. She had to be sure. If it was her missing husband, somehow he had also made the jump – but would be dead in a matter of just a couple of weeks.

Nechochwen never ceased to amaze Bethany. He knew she was trying to identify someone in the village. When they were near enough to see the net mender's shanty, he magically produced a spyglass from his waist pouch.

"Where did you get that?" Bethany asked.

"From a shipwreck, near the Devil's Stepping Stones," he replied.

Her studies of nautical history were coming back into the forefront of her memories. She knew the device was invented in the first decade of the 17th Century and quickly became available across Europe after improvements by Galileo. She also knew that it became standard equipment on most seagoing vessels within the next two decades, most predominantly on Dutch and French ships.

"Was it a Dutch ship?" she asked Nechochwen.

"It wasn't English," he answered. "We did not have contact with any living sailors from the ship. They all must have been lost at sea."

Once again, her knowledge of history took over. Dutch… what appeared to be Long Island Sound… New Amsterdam… Possibly a ship of the Dutch West India Company. It all made sense.

"May I see it, please, Nechochwen?"

"Certainly. It is why I brought it along. It does not work for us in the forest. There are too many trees to see clearly. But across open ground or open water, the eye can see more than just the trees," he said.

Crouching down behind a hogshead, Bethany trained the spyglass on the net mender's shack. It took her a minute to focus on the couple seated on the stools in front of a pile of nets. She watched as the man took off his hat and stood to stretch. As he turned first to the left and then to the right, Bethany got a clear look at his face and got weak in the knees.

"I'll be damned," she mumbled, "it's Jonathan, just like I thought. I can clearly see the scar on his chin from that shrapnel wound he got in his last firefight…"

"What did you say?" Nechochwen asked.

"Nothing important… but I know that man, the one mending the nets," she explained.

Next, she trained the spyglass on the woman who was sitting next to Jonathan. Once he sat down, she stood up, touched his shoulder, and turned towards the privy about 50 yards away. In profile, Bethany was certain she saw the telltale signs of pregnancy, noticing the prominence of what people in her time called a "baby bump." Bethany became even more unsteady than she already was. Was the woman Jonathan's wife?

"Bethany, you don't look well," Nechochwen said, his concern evident.

"I need to sit down for a moment. Do you have any water?" she asked.

"Yes, of course," he replied, passing her a water bag made from a goatskin.

After a few minutes of sitting quietly and absorbing what she had just seen, Bethany asked Nechochwen if there was a church nearby.

"Yes, there is. It was built not long after the first English came to this area."

"Will you take me there?" she asked. "It is important for me to see it."

"It's a short walk from here, but yes," Nechochwen replied.

"Good. I need to leave this place," she said, her tone suddenly dark.

As Nechochwen said, the church was only a short walk away from the wharf. The building, or at least the shell of it, looked new. The stones were unweathered and there was no moss growing in the mortar joints between them. The wooden shingles on the roof were still green and oozing sap.

When they walked around to the northeast corner of the building, the customary place for a cornerstone, Bethany saw the inscribed year: 1645. She had been here before… or was that… will be here in the future? She was becoming more and more confused and agitated with each discovery.

On a notice board, which was really nothing more than a large wooden shingle suspended between two uprights, Bethany noticed a couple of handwritten documents. They were similar in appearance, having been written in the same educated hand. After reading the first one, she had no interest in reading the second.

"I publish the banns of marriage between Mister Jonathan Harris and the widow Dorcas Parham Pinkerton, both of Newhaven. This is the first reading of the banns. If any of you know cause or just impediment why these two persons are not to be joined together in Holy Matrimony, you are to declare it forthwith."

Reverend Padraig MacKendrie

This 16th Day of June in the Year of Our Lord 1658

"Nechochwen, do you know what today's date is?" Bethany asked in a rising panic.

"It is June 20 by the English calendar," he answered.

"That sonofabitch!" Bethany mumbled to herself. "He's getting married. I am guessing it is because she is pregnant."

Forcing back tears, she turned back to Nechochwen. "Please take me back to the village now. I must speak with Aiyana."

*   *   *   *   *

Once again, it was a day where things just seemed a out of kilter. I had been sitting on my stool working on one of the larger nets when my peripheral vision caught the flash of a reflection. It was like the sun reflecting off a sniper's scope – which I knew was not possible as telescopic sights would not be invented for nearly another hundred years. Even so, it made the hair on the back of my neck stand up.

My combat experience had taught me that I should not acknowledge the threat by turning towards it; rather that I should nonchalantly move in a normal way to seek protective cover. Instead, I ignored my instincts and continued working. Dorcas noticed my uneasiness once again.

"Jonathan, this is the second time in a week that something has happened to make you as jittery as a bride on her wedding night," Dorcas teased.

"I saw something over by the warehouse that seemed out of place," I answered.

"You mean the Indian woman with the telescope?"

"So *that's* what it was!" I exclaimed in reply; inside, I was thinking, *"Why would an Indian woman be observing me like that?"*

"She left very quickly, as if she were frightened," said Dorcas. "An Indian man took her by the arm and led her away."

I had to get to the bottom of this mystery. Why were the Quinnipiac so interested in my presence? Was it the entire band or just a couple of individuals? I was confused and, unusually, a little bit frightened for my safety. The Quinnipiac were known for their stealth as stalkers, and it would be quite easy for one of them to sneak up on me at night and cut my throat as I lay in bed sleeping.

In the 21st Century, I relied on technology for the most part. Its assistance allowed me to sleep quite soundly at night in hostile areas with no one other than my spotter nearby. This was entirely different. I could not rely on Dorcas and did not want to endanger her… our child. It was my duty to protect *her*, not the other way around.

"Dorcas, do you know how to shoot?" I asked. I was pretty sure she did. "Puritan" did not mean "pacifist." The Pequot War two decades earlier proved the mettle of the Puritan settlers. They could – and would – defend themselves.

Puzzled by the question, Dorcas replied, "Yes, I do. Every English settler, man and woman alike, here in the Connecticut Colony knows how to handle a weapon. A pistol is my preference as a long gun like a rifle is too difficult for me to handle."

"I am not sure why, but I am afraid that the Indians are stalking like a deer me for some reason. I had hoped it would never come to this, but I think we should arm ourselves. Knives will not be enough against an intruder into our home.

*   *   *   *   *

Nechochwen pointed Bethany in the direction of the "women's lodge" where Aiyana had spent the past three days. He would not get close to the lodge as it was not proper for men to associate with women when they were bleeding. Bethany would be on her own. At first, she could barely see the lodge in the forest, but once she was standing next to it, she quickly found the entrance.

"Aiyana, I must speak with you," Bethany called out.

"I am here, Bethany. I will come out and sit with you for awhile," Aiyana responded. "Only women like me can come inside."

The two women were separated in age by more than three decades. Regardless, Bethany had taken Aiyana as a friend and confidante. She felt she could tell her Quinnipiac hostess anything, even things that were bizarre and troubling.

"Aiyana, when I was in the fishing village today, Nechochwen let me use his spyglass."

"What did you see?" Aiyana queried. "It had to be something terrible to upset you so."

"Uhh… I… well… I saw my… *husband* sitting with another woman and she was with child," Bethany blurted out as the tears started to flow. "It was obvious to me that they were in love. Then we walked past the church and the banns of marriage had been posted. The first reading was this past Sunday."

"Slow down, Bethany. You are breathing like a horse coming in at full gallop. What do you want to do about it?" Aiyana asked.

"I don't know…" Bethany totally lost her composure and fell into Aiyana's arms, weeping heavily. The entire time, Aiyana held Bethany close and stroked her hair. Bethany felt as comforted as if she had been in her own mother's arms after confiding about the unrequited love of a teen crush.

When Bethany regained her composure, she realized that her relationship with Pierre Delacroix had been based purely on lust and a way of meeting a visceral physical need. No matter how she sliced it, she was still madly in love with her husband, Jonathan, and had no intention of sharing him with anyone in any century. She didn't care if his current love interest… Dorcas Parham Pinkerton… was pregnant or not. She didn't care if Jonathan had been missing for three years. She had no intention of spending the rest of her life with Pierre. She shared a child with Jonathan, something that she would *never* share with Pierre.

Chapter Twenty-One: Plans
June 1658

Bethany was not quite sure what she wanted to do about the situation with Jonathan. She was afraid that a knee-jerk reaction would not be in her best interests and could trap her permanently in the 17th Century. Though she had accepted that as a likelihood and had found Nechochwen to be suitable as a potential husband, her attraction to him could not supplant her love for Jonathan.

What Bethany did know was that Pierre was no longer of interest to her as a romantic partner. If she had to choose between Pierre and Nechochwen, the Quinnipiac would win hands down. Her potential union with Nechochwen was predicated on the outcome of whatever it was she was going to do about Jonathan's presence – and Dorcas Parham Pinkerton.

Aiyana probably was not the best person to ask for advice. Her world view was limited by her age. Though she was wise beyond her years as a confidante, Bethany felt more comfortable asking Grandmother Chepi for advice, through Aiyana as translator. Bethany also wondered if perhaps Chepi knew something of visitors from other worlds and simply had not yet shared that knowledge.

Aiyana would be returning from the women's lodge for the morning meal. Bethany knew Aiyana's time at the lodge was ending and that she would have a translator for her imminent conversation with Chepi. It would, however, have to wait until an appropriate time.

Aiyana returned to the main village with a broad smile on her face. She knew that she had to keep Bethany's spirits up in light of her discovery the previous day.

"Good morning, Bethany!" Aiyana said cheerfully as she approached the cooking fire where Bethany was stirring the porridge.

"Aiyana! I am so glad you are back with us," Bethany responded. "Once the morning meal is complete, I need you to help me speak with Grandmother Chepi. I really need the advice of an older woman."

Aiyana looked disappointed at this revelation. She understood but was hurt by Bethany's recognition of the age difference. Bethany had become Aiyana's closest friend in the past few weeks and they had shared nearly everything with each other.

"As you wish, my friend," Aiyana said curtly.

"I am so sorry, Aiyana, but I don't think you have enough experience for my situation. There are things I haven't told you and can only share with someone having Chepi's wisdom," Bethany explained, sensing the hurt in Aiyana's voice.

* * * * *

Our wedding was just a little more than two weeks away. After the third reading of the banns of marriage, we intended for the ceremony to take place the following day around noon. Time was no longer on our side as I was already seeing Dorcas's "baby bump." If I could see it, other people could certainly seeing it as well. The men were always indifferent to such things, but I wondered what the women of the village were saying when Dorcas and I were out of earshot.

I could hear the conversations in my head: "I heard they have to get married…" "She's a strumpet, for sure!" "The most eligible man in town and he picks *her*?"

One thing that Dorcas and I had to worry about was the wedding feast. Neither of us had any family (*of course, I didn't: they hadn't even been born yet!*) and I was uncertain of the customs of the day. Were weddings free-for-alls, or was there a guest list? I had to find out so that I could manage my own expectations for the event.

"Dorcas, who comes to weddings?" I asked as we worked together on one of the larger nets. "In the Virginia Colony, they usually filled the church and had a feast afterwards."

"It is not very different here," Dorcas responded, "the church will be full and there will be a picnic feast on the village green after the ceremony. The men will be doing plenty of drinking."

I had been thinking that I wanted Fatou to attend as well. She was still in New Haven, now enslaved to the Selectmen of the town. In essence, she was town property. As a healer, she was responsible for the health and welfare of the slaves in the pens until they were sold. She was also the reason that Dorcas was still alive after her flogging.

"Do you think it would be possible for Fatou to attend as well?" I asked.

"The townfolk will frown on slaves attending. She might not be allowed inside the church, but certainly she will be permitted to attend the feast," Dorcas answered.

"I wish there was some way we could get her freedom. She is the only reason you are still alive, my dear, and carrying our child. If it were not for her skills as a healer, you would have died a feverish death from infection."

"Jonathan, my love, I know full well what the consequences would have been without Fatou. I shall speak to the Reverend MacKendrie myself and ask him to intercede with the Selectmen on our behalf. I see no reason they will not grant our wish."

Dorcas had become the model Christian since her recovery, at least on the surface. She did from time to time tell me how little she got out of the Reverend's sermons and how she found Sunday services a colossal inconvenience. Had church attendance not been mandatory for everyone but the one Jewish family in town, she likely would not have had a record of perfect attendance.

"Besides, Jonathan, I haven't exactly been pure," she teased. "This bump in my belly proves how impure I really have been, but I do love you so."

It was the middle of the day, and the harbor was bustling with people. I wanted to take Dorcas into my arms but instead opted for a tender squeeze of her hand. It was the most proper of my options; what I really wanted was to take her back to my cottage and ravish her. That would have to wait until later.

As luck would have it, Reverend MacKendrie and his wife, Penelope, were strolling through the harbor on their way to the fish market. It would not have been proper for a pastor's wife to wander through the town without either her husband or a female companion. As most women treated her as they did Dorcas, with indifference, whenever Penelope went out, Reverend MacKendrie was right there with her.

"Good day to you, Reverend and Goody MacKendrie!" I called out as they approached.

The Reverend tipped his hat in acknowledgement. "Good day to you as well, Mister Harris and Widow Pinkerton. You have been in our prayers of late."

At this point, Dorcas chimed in. "Goody MacKendrie, might I have a moment of your time?"

"Yes, certainly," Penelope MacKendrie replied.

I knew what Dorcas was going to discuss with the Reverend's wife. She needed someone to stand for her at the wedding. We had discussed this very issue before our dinner with them a couple of months earlier and it was time to put that plan into motion. From the smile on Penelope MacKendrie's face and the bearhug she received from Dorcas, I knew that all was well.

"Mister Harris, do you have someone to stand for you as well?" MacKendrie asked.

The only person I could think of was Captain Palmer, of the *Desire*. He had recently retired from going to sea and instead was involved in coordinating the slave auctions. Both enterprises had served him well financially and I knew that he was now a man of considerable wealth.

"Reverend, I am going to ask Captain Palmer to stand for me at the wedding. He was responsible for my rescue on the high seas and helped me become accustomed to life here in New Haven." Now all I had to do was locate and ask Palmer.

"Good, good. An appropriate choice," MacKendrie replied, "do not forget that the second reading of your banns is this Sunday. Good day." He tipped his hat and turned to rejoin his wife.

"Good day to you as well, Reverend," I responded, tipping my own hat in reply.

*   *   *   *   *

Bethany finally had worked up the nerve to speak with Chepi. With Aiyana by her side, they entered Chepi's lodge and took respectful seats near her small fire.

"Grandmother Chepi," Bethany began with Aiyana translating, "I came to this village from far away. I do not know how I got here nor if I will ever be able to return to my home."

Chepi held up her hand as a signal for Bethany to stop talking. Bethany was puzzled by the old woman's response. It was as if she was reading Bethany's mind.

In slightly accented English, Chepi spoke, "My child, I know from where you have come – "

"You speak English?" Bethany interrupted with a tone of surprise in her voice.

"You never asked. Instead, you relied on my granddaughter to speak for you, and she has done that very well. May I continue?"

"Yes, Grandmother, please," said Bethany.

"You have come from another land and another time," Chepi explained. "You are not simply lost in place; you are lost in time as well."

Bethany's puzzled look drew a smile from Chepi.

"Child," Chepi continued, "you are not the first and will not be the last." Chepi's status in the tribe afforded her the privilege of calling everyone "child," regardless of their age. She was well aware that Bethany was only a couple of years younger.

"Can I return to my own time?" Bethany asked.

"It is not impossible," Chepi said. "It must happen when there is no moon."

"Do you know when that will be?" Bethany asked.

"In about two weeks, at the end of the month you call 'June'," Chepi responded.

"That's right after the third reading of the banns..." Bethany said as her eyes met Aiyana's.

Turning back to Chepi, Bethany asked, "Grandmother, what must I do to make it happen?"

"Do you remember were Aiyana found you, and the circle carved into the tree?"

"Yes, Grandmother. I remember."

"You must be there precisely at sunset and remain until midnight. It can only be you and one other person."

"That means I can take Jonathan with me?" Bethany's eyes brightened with the thought of taking her husband home to meet his son.

"Who is this 'Jonathan' of whom you speak?"

"He is… was… my husband in my time. We have a son, Grandmother. We thought he was lost at sea. Now he is betrothed to a widow in town, and she is with child. They are to be married at the end of the month, June, when you say it might be possible for me to return home."

"The Quinnipiac people do not get involved in the affairs of the white settlers," Chepi declared. "It is up to you to do what you must to return home with your husband." Chepi looked briefly into the fire before continuing, "The circle carved into the tree is the key to your return. You must follow these instructions exactly."

"Yes, Grandmother?" Bethany's tone made it clear that she wanted Chepi to continue.

"The person you take with you must be touching you at all times or they will be left behind." Chepi was careful not to specify that other person as Jonathan. She knew that he had apparently not come to this time the same way that Bethany had, putting his ability to return in doubt.

"Yes, Grandmother," Bethany acknowledged.

"Put the pointer finger of your right hand at the very top of the circle. You must hold it very still until you are sure the circle recognizes you are there."

"How will I know that, Grandmother?"

"You will know. It is different for everyone."

"What then, after that?"

"Trace the outer ring of the circle with your pointer finger. Slowly. You must go all the way around like the hands on a clock. Not backwards, as you are going forward to your time."

Bethany suddenly made the connection between the 360 degrees in a circle and the fact that she had jumped back in time by exactly that number of years. She wondered if she could stop the trace of her finger three degrees short of a full circle and return to 2015, before the time Jonathan went missing. Could she thus prevent his disappearance?

Chepi brought Bethany out of her daze. "I know what you are thinking, Child. That you could chose the time to which you would return. It is not like that. A circle is meant to be complete. Not broken into parts."

"Yes, Grandmother."

"Once you have gone all the way around the circle, you must place your hands in the center, with your left hand over your right. If you have done everything correctly, you will travel to your own time."

Chepi continued, "It will seem like it is taking a lifetime to get there and you will see other people along the way. Do not worry. When you get to the end of your journey, you will know."

"Grandmother, I am very tired now. May I go back to my hut and sleep?" Bethany asked. Chepi nodded her assent.

Chapter Twenty-Two: Dreams
Late June 1658

Aiyana escorted Bethany back to their hut. On the way, it seemed as if Bethany was elsewhere and detached from reality. Aiyana knew that it would be a rough night, as the Grandmother's instructions always made it difficult for time travelers to remain asleep. They often had nightmares, night terrors, really, that literally tore their minds apart, leaving them incoherent and confused when they awoke in the morning. Aiyana hoped that Bethany would be different.

Within minutes after crawling under the bearskin robe, Bethany was fast asleep. She was exhausted. Aiyana took that as her cue to sleep as well; banking the fire for the night, she joined her friend under the bearskin. It was a cool early summer evening, still cool enough that the combination of the bearskin and the warm body of a bedmate made it more comfortable than being alone. Besides, the fire would soon be out and there would only be body heat for warmth.

As the night wore on, Bethany began to dream. The first dream, not more than an hour after they had gone to bed, was terrifying. Bethany awoke with a start, tearing the bearskin robe away from Aiyana as well.

In her dream, Bethany had seen that Dorcas woman giving birth. Not just as a casual observer, but as a full-fledged participant, up close and personal. Bethany watched as the baby descended through Dorcas's birth canal; it was certainly more than she wanted to see. First the head was born, then the shoulders… and with one final push, the baby was born. A boy, to be named Benjamin Harris as Bethany had seen on Jonathan's tombstone.

Bethany's unconscious mind was trying to figure out why Jonathan's name would have been on a tombstone if she had been able to take him back to 2018. If he disappeared with her in the woods, at the circle, would the townspeople hold a memorial service for him? Were there other time travelers in New Haven who would stop at nothing to see a burial take place – with a body that was not Jonathan's? It was like she was a contestant on a TV quiz show: "I'll take 'No Rhyme Nor Reason' for 200, please."

The dreams came every hour or so and Aiyana did her best to comfort Bethany when the dreams disturbed her. When she did awaken mid-dream, Bethany was usually able to recount in minute detail what she had "seen." The dreams seemed to alternate between variations of Dorcas in childbirth and Jonathan's tombstone.

Just before dawn, Bethany had one last dream. This time, the story was completely different. It was a wedding ceremony. From the narthex, Bethany observed as a shroud of smoke cleared to reveal Jonathan standing before the chancel with the minister – who her dream presumed to be the Reverend Padraig MacKendrie – and a man dressed in a sea captain's uniform waiting for the bride to come down the aisle.

As dreams often do, Bethany's perspective changed; she turned slightly to her left and saw Dorcas standing next to her in a loose-fitting gown. In the dream, the "baby bump" was hidden by the loose-fitting material, but Bethany knew it was there. The wedding could not have waited even another week before it would have been almost impossible to hide Dorcas's expanding waist and bust lines.

Fully awake at sunrise, Bethany confided in Aiyana, "I know what I must do. I have to stop the wedding. Jonathan may be the father of Dorcas's child, but he is already married to me."

"But that time is in the future," Aiyana replied. "Can you hold him to honor vows that will not be said for many years?"

"I am here and he is here. It does not matter when the vows take… took… place. He is my husband and the father of our son," Bethany argued. "The marriage cannot go forward. I must take him back to our own time."

"Grandmother Chepi said it was possible for you to take another with you from the circle. You intend for it to be Jonathan… What is your plan to get him to the circle?" Aiyana asked.

"I have not yet decided," Bethany answered.

*　　*　　*　　*　　*

I was amazed at how simple it was to arrange a wedding in Puritan times. No overbearing wedding planner. No photographer or videographer. No caterer. Weddings in the 17th Century were community celebrations. Everything was simply done, with friends and neighbors all adding to the festivities with food, decorations, libations, or music. It seemed that everyone had a unique skill and that Dorcas and I would be married in style – without spending huge sums of money.

Everything was falling into place. Captain Palmer agreed to stand by me as witness, as had Goody MacKendrie for Dorcas. With Dorcas's background, and especially her very public punishment, having the pastor's wife as a witness would give Dorcas a little more credibility in the community. I had noticed quite some time ago that pastors and their wives were put on the pedestal of virtue.

I had also appealed to the Selectmen to give Fatou permission to attend as well. At first, they were somewhat reluctant, with Fatou being a slave. After I explained to them the unique role Fatou had played in Dorcas's recovery, they gave their assent. "However, She will not be allowed to participate in the wedding feast, though. That privilege is reserved for freemen," I was told.

Our work done for the day, Dorcas and I retired to her cottage for dinner. We had gotten into the habit of making sure that the shutters remained open so that curiosity-seekers could see that nothing untoward was happening. *"That,"* I mused to myself, *"would come later…"*

Dorcas was a wonderful cook. Though she had been busy all day mending nets with me, she still managed to put dinner on the table without much ado, keeping things simple. Our usual meal was fish fresh from the boat and root vegetables from her cellar, cooked together in a cast iron cauldron suspended from hook over the fire, all perfectly seasoned. I never grew tired of such delectable fare and I was certainly eating better than I did when I was cooking for myself – before Dorcas and I became a couple.

Dinner finished, I would make it a point to leave her cottage by the front door, pausing in the doorway for visual effect. As a courtesy, I would also close her shutters for the night. I wanted as many passers-by as possible to see my departure. From there, I would go directly to my cottage nearer the marsh and waterfront, close all the shutters, and prepare for bed (or so I wanted people to think!).

Over time, we had developed a rather elaborate ruse that would allow me to return to Dorcas's cottage undetected. The marsh behind my cottage was passable on foot except at extreme high tide. Because of the livestock fences separating the properties between my cottage and Dorcas's, I was obscured from view and could easily enter her back garden near the privy.

Once I was finally inside her cottage, we would literally attack each other with pent-up lust, eventually falling asleep in each other's arms. By morning, when the clock on her mantel chimed 5:00, I would awaken and return to my own cottage, always alert for other early risers who might suspect that I had spent the night someplace other than my own home.

As the day of our wedding got closer, I began to experience some rather bizarre dreams. I was concerned that none of those dreams included an identifiable Dorcas; rather, it was Bethany's face that always seemed to appear from a phantasm. My dreams reminded me of any of several Broadway shows or movies popular in the 20th and 21st Centuries, with the haunting phantasms appearing out of thin air.

Why was I seeing Bethany in my dreams? Was the impression she had made on my psyche' so pervasive that I would not ever be able to be happily married to another woman? It was all a mystery, one that intensified with each dream-filled night.

Thankfully, I had not fully awakened during any of the dreams, leaving Dorcas undisturbed. The last thing I needed was to explain to her that I was dreaming about another woman. The only details I had ever given Dorcas about my previous marriage was that my wife had died in childbirth. That I was dreaming about my first wife was the last thing Dorcas would want to hear. The phrase "Hell hath no fury…" had taken on a new meaning with Dorcas's pregnancy.

Still, I needed to resolve the emotional conflict I was facing. Could I be happy with Dorcas? Would I eventually forget Bethany? Or… was it more likely that I would be haunted by the memory of my last night with Bethany on the foredeck of the "Great Escape?" Only time would tell.

The mantel clock struck five a.m. and I rose, dressed, and returned to my cottage to prepare for the day ahead. On the way into my back garden, I stopped at the privy then went into the small chicken coop to see if I might retrieve an egg or two for breakfast. My handful of laying hens had been exceeding expectations of late and I was never lacking for fresh eggs. What I couldn't use, Dorcas would use in one of her delectable dishes.

After starting my cooking fire and setting my skillet nearby to preheat, I used my razor-sharp kitchen knife to carve a chunk of meat from the cured ham that hung from the rafters in my rudimentary kitchen. I made sure that the meat had plenty of fat, as that would be necessary to grease my skillet and keep the eggs from sticking.

The ham hit the hot skillet with a satisfying sizzle and the fat immediately began rendering from the meat, quickly greasing the pan for my eggs. Using only the residual heat in the iron skillet, the eggs cooked perfectly. *"Just like I used to cook for Bethany,"* I thought.

Why was Bethany's memory taking over my thoughts and my dreams? She was haunting me from 360 years in the future. I could offer no rational explanation, but I also was not in a particularly rational situation.

When I met Dorcas later that morning at our netmending shanty, she noticed right away that I was preoccupied with something. I didn't want to open the conversation, so I remained silent until she was ready to speak.

"Jonathan, you were restless last night. Do you remember any of your dreams?" Dorcas asked.

"Everything was fuzzy," I answered. "It was as if I was outside my body looking down at the world." A lie, but it was all I could think of in the moment.

"I hope that once we are married and our child is born, the dreams will stop," Dorcas said, trying to console me.

I looked at her and smiled. Inside, though, I was tied up in knots. All of my time in combat and in the hospital after being wounded did not leave me with any Post-Traumatic Stress Disorder. I managed to escape the effects that some of my teammates had experienced – then – but now, I was having *pre*-stress symptoms that were quite unnerving.

Chapter Twenty-Three: Almost Time
June 22-23, 1658

Just after dawn on Saturday, June 22, the Quinnipiacs were disturbed by a group of about a dozen white men and their barking dogs loudly coming into the village. They were demanding the release of a white woman who, by their account, was "being held against her will." It was obvious that the men were fueled by copious amounts of home-brewed liquid courage.

Their approach to the village was anything but stealthy and they had alerted every Quinnipiac man well in advance, allowing them to steal away and conceal themselves in the surrounding woodlands. By the time the white men were in the center of the village, every bow was nocked and arrows ready to be loosed in defense of the Quinnipiac families. It would have been a quick and easy fight – with the Quinnipiacs winning the battle decisively.

Only Chepi's foresight prevented a bloodbath. She knew that if her band killed even a single settler, they would be attacked mercilessly and either exterminated or driven entirely from the area. It was up to her to defuse the situation and restore calm.

The leader of the white mob harangued Chepi, "We know you heathens have one of ours here. She's being kept against her will. No civilized white woman would want to stay with the likes of you by their own accord!"

With Aiyana standing beside her, Chepi reached inside her deerskin shirt and pulled out a hand-carved cross from her cleavage, brandishing it as if it were a protective weapon. "Good sir, I must remind you that we are a mostly Christian village. My people were brought into your faith at the end of the Pequot War twenty years ago by Reverend Eaton, who also taught us your language."

"So says you!" the leader bellowed back in a hateful tone.

"Our Lord Jesus Christ said, 'love thy neighbor as thyself,'" Chepi said calmly. "We are your neighbors, not your enemies."

Once again, the mob's leader spoke derisively, "If you are not holding her against her will, let her come forth and declare it to be true."

Bethany had been standing behind Chepi and Aiyana the entire time. Dressed like her Quinnipiac friends, the mob had assumed she was "one of them" and not a white woman. The mob believed that any self-respecting white woman would be appropriately attired, and that did not include buckskin garments.

As she pushed between Aiyana and Chepi, Bethany whispered, "Grandmother… Aiyana… I will speak to them, but I will not use my real name."

Stepping out into the open, Bethany addressed the mob. "Yes, Grandmother Chepi is correct. I am here of my own free will and am not a captive. I choose to be here among these fine people."

"What is your name, then?" the mob leader demanded.

"My name is not important. They do not call me '*Maconaquea*', the White Captive, and that is all you need to know."

"You've taken a heathen name?" the leader demanded.

Bethany paused for a moment to consider her next words very carefully. "Yes, but it was earned. I am one of them now," Bethany replied as she took both Chepi's and Aiyana's hands. "I am now known as '*Shaniya*' or 'She who is on her own way.' I no longer wish to use my birth name."

"You have heard her words, gentlemen. I suggest you be on your way," Chepi said dismissively.

"You've not heard the last of us, old woman! Don't you go hidin' any more white women for yer men to have their way with," the mob leader said as the group turned and left.

Once the mob was out of earshot, Bethany broke down and cried. After regaining her composure, she hugged Chepi and Aiyana, telling them that "you are my family now."

*   *   *   *   *

Reverend MacKendrie's sermon on Sunday, June 23, the Second Sunday after Pentecost on the Liturgical Calendar focused on the Epistle for the day, specifically Galatians 3:26-27:

"For ye are all the children of God by faith in Christ Jesus. For as many of you as have been baptized into Christ have put on Christ."

MacKendrie made sure that he mentioned the conversion of a good share of the Quinnipiacs to Christianity and their baptisms. Many of the slaves, too, had chosen to follow Christian teachings; even Fatou was accepting Christian ways. "By their faith," he said, "they are as much a part of the Kingdom of God as any of you who have come to this new land from England with generations of faith behind you." I noticed several men squirming uncomfortably in their pews as the good Reverend spoke.

*　*　*　*　*

Outside the church, Bethany, Chepi, Aiyana, and Nechochwen could clearly hear Reverend MacKendrie's stentorian voice as he delivered the sermon. They could only smile at each other, as his message mirrored Chepi's challenge to the mob that had visited their village the day before. How he had become aware of the stand-off between Chepi and the mob was a mystery. Bethany surmised, correctly so, that at least one man in the group had a conscience and had secretly given the good Reverend the information.

At the end of the service, Bethany heard the second reading of the banns. It made her weak at the knees, wobbly enough that Aiyana and Nechochwen had to support her. There was little she could do to object to the banns without giving herself away, and she had not yet developed an escape plan should she decide to announce her objection to the marriage.

The service now over, the Quinnipiac group had to quickly and quietly blend back into the woods. They were not welcome in or near the settler's church, though they had professed their Christian faith. Slaves, on the other hand, were allowed to enter and sit or stand in the narthex.

*   *   *   *   *

I hadn't realized that there was tension between the local tribe and the white settlers. A rumor had started that their leader, Chepi, was holding a white woman hostage in their village and some of the less tolerant men of New Haven were set on rescuing her and had in fact assembled a raiding party the day before.

Totally unaware, I was so focused on our imminent wedding and Dorcas that I had neglected to keep my focus on my surroundings. I had lost my "situational awareness" and had forgotten my training. If this were a hostile situation, it would have ended badly for me.

At the end of the service, Reverend MacKendrie read our banns of marriage for the second time. As with the first, there were no objections from the congregation. It was now one week and a day before Dorcas and I would be husband and wife.

All of the wedding plans were coming together. Dorcas's wedding dress had been sewn by one of the slave women that several households shared as a seamstress. Everybody in town was contributing something, even the harpies who had wrongfully accused Dorcas of gossiping. Personally, I was looking forward to the spit-roasted hog that one of the farmers was contributing. We had been eating so much fish that I wanted some variety in my diet.

Dorcas laughed out loud when I told her about the hog, then told me why she was laughing. "You know you aren't going to have much time to eat, my dear. It is customary for the groom to speak with everyone at the feast and it is not polite to talk with your mouth full."

"As always, my darling, you are right. I shall be sure to eat a hearty breakfast that morning and be careful about what I drink after the ceremony. I don't think you would want your new husband falling drunkenly asleep on your wedding night, would you?" My suggestive tone brought a crimson flush across her face.

"Jonathan Harris!" Dorcas scolded, "someone might hear you!"

"Everyone knows we are going to be married, so I shouldn't have to be so careful about what people think," I told her.

"You do remember what brought us together in the first place, do you not?" Dorcas teased; the memory of her hanging limp, almost naked, and nearly lifeless from the whipping post left me speechless.

"Can we think about more pleasant things?" I asked in a tone that was meant to discourage her from continuing.

"Yes, my darling," Dorcas answered, ending that line of conversation.

Sunday afternoons, weather permitting, were social affairs. Families shared meals on the village green. Children were allowed to run free. The women bustled about, making sure that everyone was fed. The men drank ale and smoked. Conversations were about anything and everything, and I overheard more than a couple of women talking about Dorcas's apparent reform since her whipping.

"That Mister Harris is making a respectable woman out of her," I heard one woman say, *sotto voce*, to her group. Another woman brought the group to giggles as she openly described her imagination of what would transpire on our wedding night.

The men, on the other hand, were less likely to discuss the dynamics of social relationships. Instead, they spoke of the goings-on in England and how Oliver Cromwell had dissolved the Second Protectorate Parliament. The news had just reached the colonies, though the dissolution had taken place in February. I wondered how anyone could keep up with "current" events back in England with a months-long ocean crossing delaying the arrival of news.

There was much more discussion of the written constitution, officially called the Instrument of Government, which authorized elections for the House of Commons but excluded Royalists and Catholics from the vote. Other aspects of the Instrument I recognized as cornerstone precepts of the form of government that would, in about 130 years, become the United States of America. Here I was, living the history that I had only read about in my other life.

These Sunday gatherings over the past four years were where I had also learned that the term "Puritan" had nothing to do with an avoidance of pleasure; rather, that it was a purely religious term aimed at completing the

English Reformation and fully separating from Roman Catholic practices. The Puritan culture of the northern colonies expected people to engage in pleasurable activities (including sex, but only in the context of marriage), a far cry from how H. L. Mencken had defined the Puritan movement in his writings of the 1940s.

I knew from the Sunday gatherings that once Dorcas and I were married, the fact that we enjoyed each other physically was nothing to be ashamed of nor hidden. The reality, I learned, was that Puritan men and women both openly discussed their marital exploits, albeit within gender-segregated groups. There were just some things that men did not talk about with a woman that was not his wife.

Chapter Twenty-Four: Sleepless
June 24-25, 1658

Bethany was sleep-deprived and to the point of hallucinating. There were times she could not separate her awake times and her sleep times. Her periods of hypnopompia and hypnogogia were merging and had she been in the 21st Century, she could have consulted with a professional. The best that the white settlers in 1658 would be able to offer was "shall we pray about it?" and the best Chepi would offer was time in a sweat lodge.

She was still wrestling with how to deal with Jonathan and his betrothed. Timing, she knew, was everything. If she was to get Jonathan back, she had to be bold and decisive. Giving him time to think would just complicate the situation. *"And I don't give a fuck about Dorcas,"* she mumbled to herself.

Chepi sensed that something was wrong with Bethany. Her movements had become perfunctory, and it seemed as if there was no joy in her life.

"Bethany, my child, what is troubling you?" Chepi asked once they were alone.

"I know that Jonathan is to be married one week from today. I don't know what to do. I dream about Jonathan when I fall asleep and in the morning, I awaken from a dream that seems to have lasted the entire night. Grandmother, can you help me?"

"If you had lived here your entire life," Chepi began, "we would send you out into the wilderness to search for plants we can eat. Because you came from another world, another time, you do not know what plants to look for. It is knowledge that is passed down from mother to daughter."

"Are you telling me that time alone is what I truly need?" Bethany asked.

"Yes, child. You need time apart, but it has to mean something. Wandering aimlessly in the forest alone could be dangerous and you would naturally keep thinking about… Jonathan and Dorcas."

"Is there anything I can do right here in the village?" Bethany asked.

"There should be no one in the 'women's lodge' for three days. You can go there, and Aiyana will help you turn it into a sweat lodge. Aiyana will leave you there alone. You must remain awake to keep it always warm; you cannot let the fire die for the entire three days. If you do that, the demons inside your head will leave and your mind will be clear. Then and only then will you be able to see a clear path forward."

"Grandmother, you are wise. When Aiyana comes back from the river, I will ask her to help me." Bethany was still skeptical that private meditation would lead her to a solution. It was the best thing she had right now and continuing with the hallucinations and nightmares was enough to drive her totally mad.

Aiyana returned to the village just after mid-day. Bethany immediately took her friend aside and explained what Chepi had suggested. Aiyana's response was immediate and affirmative.

"I would be honored to help you with your first spirit journey," Aiyana said as she gently took both of Bethany's hands in her own. "We will start tomorrow as soon as the sun comes over the horizon."

Bethany felt as if a huge weight had been removed from her shoulders. Knowing that she was taking charge of her own emotional state and at least trying to do something about her plight was intrinsically comforting. When she was in the Navy, she had been a regular practitioner of yoga. She especially enjoyed an extended *savasana* at the end of a practice.

With a plan of action now in place, Bethany's mood improved considerably. Nechochwen had been avoiding her since Sunday services; he did not wish to intrude nor cause her any additional pain. Like Aiyana, he saw an immediate change in Bethany's demeanor and decided that the time was right to speak with her again.

"Bethany, I know you wish to be true to Jonathan. If that cannot be, I would be honored if you would accept me as your new husband," Nechochwen said solemnly.

"Nechochwen, I cannot give you an answer until I know myself what is to be. After the next reading of the banns and his wedding to Dorcas, I might be able to give you the answer you seek," she replied.

Nechochwen nodded in understanding, patted Bethany on the shoulder, and headed towards the running brook in search of the elusive trout that lived there.

*   *   *   *   *

With exactly one week until our wedding, I was getting more and more nervous. Visions of Bethany still haunted me day and night and there were times when I saw her face on Dorcas's body. Was this an otherworldly message someone was trying to send me or was I just nervous about being married again? I needed to focus on something else that didn't involve Dorcas in proximity. I thought about going away for a couple of days, into the forest, and roughing it. I was no stranger to survival situations and always found them comforting – as long as no one was shooting at me or trying to slit my throat as I slept.

"Dorcas, darling, I think I need to be alone for a couple of days. The nets are all mended and the fishermen are waiting for the first signs of the summer migrations before going to sea again."

"Whatever you need to do, but please be careful. The forests around New Haven are said to be haunted," Dorcas teased, "and you could get carried away by ghosts."

I stifled a laugh at her expense. Superstitions abounded in this decade, in this century, and there was little I could do to change peoples' outlook nor their opinions. I did truly love Dorcas and wanted us to have a happy and productive life together, perhaps with a couple of children.

With Dorcas's assent, I packed my things and enough provisions for three nights in the forest, then rented a horse from the village livery. I decided to head southeast along the coast towards Fairfield, where my 21st Century research said I might have some ancestors. If my memory was correct, some of them would be alive as adults in 1658. Fairfield was about twenty-five miles away, so the horse was a necessity if I was to get there and back in three days. I was certainly up for the physical challenge; the mental gymnastics that would be required to keep my wits about me were another thing entirely.

I had not been too far away from the New Haven docks or marshes since my arrival four years earlier. It was refreshing to be away from the smells of the fishing industry: fish offal rotting in the sun, chum pots being loaded onto the boats before a day's fishing in what would become known as Long Island Sound, unwashed male bodies, and the permeating smell of salt marsh mud. My sense of smell was assailed with the smells of freshness, sometimes so intense I thought I could even smell the colors around me.

I noticed squirrels chattering in the trees, deer foraging in the undergrowth, and occasionally heard bald eagles chattering to each other. I was so absorbed in my surroundings that I almost missed the strange carving in the trunk of a tree a few yards off the woodland path. It was an unusual circle with what looked like a maze within it. I was almost certain it was some sort of Native American trail or boundary marker. Seeing no signs of human life anywhere nearby, I studied the carving for a few moments, then continued on my way.

By dead reckoning, I estimated that I was about five miles outside of Fairfield around 4 p.m. That left a few hours of daylight – enough time for me to set up camp and have a relaxing meal beside the fire. I first tied the horse to a picket line in a grassy area adjacent to my campsite. Livery horses were notorious for instinctively returning home during the night and I did not want to walk the entire distance back to New Haven.

In my "other" life, I would have had a book to read. Unfortunately, they were in short supply in the Connecticut Colony – other than the King James Bible. Printed books in the 17th Century were heavy and awkward, so the average traveler on horseback would not waste the weight; neither did I.

Instead, I decided to spend my time carving a wedding gift for Dorcas. I had seen ornate wooden spoons adorning the walls of some homes in New Haven, so I asked Reverend MacKendrie if he knew anything about them. He told me that they were called "love spoons," and were usually carved by Welsh sailors on long voyages. When they returned home, they would present the spoon to their loved one as a token of affection. I thought it was a very romantic thing to do, so I used my relaxing time after a dinner of dried venison and biscuits to begin carving such a spoon.

As the daylight waned, I realized that I was very tired and probably should turn in for the night. As it was a warm evening, I simply unrolled my blanket on top of a bed of pine boughs and drifted off to sleep.

In field situations during my career as a naval officer, I slept very lightly. Any unusual noise and I would be instantly awake. The Connecticut forests were no different. As I was not accustomed to the background noise, I woke with every rustle of a leaf, every snap of a twig... *"Wait a minute... did I just hear a twig snap?"*

I was instantly alert and slowly reached for the pistol I had hidden under the blanket near my head. I already had my knife in hand, so I was ready for just about anything. Rolling over quickly to find the source of the noise and aiming the pistol in that general direction, I was assailed with a nauseating blast of skunk. Apparently, I had startled him as much as he had startled me. The smell permeated everything. My clothes… my blanket… my hair… all now bore the sulfurous reek of skunk. I knew that this encounter would be responsible for ending my adventure as I could not go into any public place without first ridding myself of the smell – which I knew would be a challenging task. I hoped that Dorcas would know what to do. I would be on my way back to New Haven first thing in the morning and I prayed that the horse would not rebel against the odor.

*　　*　　*　　*　　*

In parallel with Jonathan's venture into the forest, Aiyana was helping Bethany turn the women's lodge into a sweat lodge, where Bethany would spend the next three days. First, they made sure that the lodge was impermeably covered with hides to keep in the heat. Next, they stacked enough firewood to last more than the three days. The preparations complete, Aiyana gave Bethany her final instructions.

"To be sure you remain in the lodge for the entire three days, you will undress and I will take your clothing with me. I will visit you once each day with a small meal and water to drink. The meal will be purposely small as time in the lodge is about denial and reflection. But you must drink every drop of water I bring for you. If you chose to end your time, you may call out to either me or the Grandmother and we will bring you your clothing."

"I'm glad you did not tell me about having to be naked while I am in the lodge," Bethany teased. She knew that it was a necessary part of the experience, to rid oneself of all external influences and focus the mind on what must be decided.

The fire was lit and the smoke rose cleanly through the vent in the roof. Inside the lodge, the temperature rose quickly. At first, Bethany enjoyed the sensation of permeating warmth. After a few hours, though, it became an oppressive heat. She ignored the heat and focused her mind on the problem at hand: Jonathan's imminent marriage to another woman.

The hours all blended together and as there was little light coming through the tanned hides, Bethany did not know if it was night or day. Her mind raced with possibilities, the ones that would bring Jonathan back to her getting the most mental attention. Other options, though they were few, were quickly discarded as unworkable or unpalatable.

With the passage of a full day, Aiyana arrived as promised, with a small meal and a goatskin water bag. Bethany was ravenous.

"Shall I sit with you for a while?" Aiyana asked.

"If that is allowed," Bethany responded.

"For our own women, it is discouraged to have a guest in the sweat lodge. You are not of our blood and may need someone to share your thoughts with," Aiyana explained.

"Please, stay if you can, Aiyana. I would like that very much."

Aiyana undressed and joined Bethany in the sweat lodge for several hours, breaking with the Quinnipiac tradition of solitude. The two women were completely at ease with each other without the encumberance of clothing.

"I must take Jonathan with me back to my own time," Bethany began. "I know how to take him with me from the circle but getting him there is another matter entirely."

"Do you need more time to think about it?" Aiyana asked.

"I certainly do," Bethany answered.

"When I come back with your meal tomorrow, I hope you will have a plan," Aiyana said as she dressed and left the lodge.

Chapter Twenty-Five: Something Smells
June 26, 1658

At dawn, I broke camp and repacked my equipment and provisions into the saddlebags. The normally affectionate mare shied away from me because of the skunk smell, but after giving her several apples, she settled down. I couldn't afford a skittish horse that would bolt at the slightest startle.

"Good girl," I cooed as I scratched her long nose, "it's not so bad, now, is it?" One more apple… I mounted up and we were on our way back home.

The closer I got to New Haven and my cottage, the more people I encountered on the road. Each time, the reaction was the same: they would cover their mouths and noses and quickly head off in a direction that did not involve passing near me. Apparently, I had gone "nose blind" to the smell: it didn't seem to bother me anymore.

I first stopped at Dorcas's cottage. I could not approach to knock on the door because I knew how bad I must smell, so I called out to her from the hitching post outside.

"Dorcas? Are you there?"

"Jonathan? You aren't due home until tomorrow at the earliest… and what on God's good earth is that smell?"

"I had an encounter with a skunk last night. He let me know for certain that I was encroaching on his territory," I answered.

"As bad as you stink, you must have gotten close enough to be sure it was a 'he'," Dorcas teased, stifling a giggle.

"I certainly did not!" I was surprised at the righteous indignation in my own tone. I needed to be rid of the smell once and for all. "Do you know how to rid oneself of skunk smell?" I asked, softening my tone considerably.

"Well, the best thing we can do for the clothing is to bury or burn it. You will just have to purchase new garments from the cloth merchant," Dorcas explained. "With your permission, I shall go to your cottage and collect a change of clothes for you." She chose her words carefully, as there were several townspeople within earshot; the last thing we needed was an accusation of impropriety this close to our wedding.

"Yes, of course. That would be wise. I shall wait for your return," I replied. "To save offending everyone's dignity, I will go into your garden and be prepared to change garments in the privacy of your chicken coop."

"You will need a bath first," she teased. "Some lavender soap should do the trick. You can change where you bathe and throw your old clothes straight into the fire."

"Lavender... did it have to be lavender?" I thought. *"I hate lavender."*

Dorcas turned on her heel and strode purposefully across the green. I could see her enter my cottage, leaving the door ajar, and knew that she knew exactly where my clothing would be found, right down to my stockings and underbreeches.

I was, however, in a quandary about the issue of bathing. It would not be proper for me to do so inside Dorcas's cottage (as much as I would have liked to!), so after she returned, I sent her to the tavern to ask if I could use their outdoor bathing area. She returned in just a few minutes with a crock of preserved tomatoes, courtesy of the tavern owner. There was a thick beeswax coating over the top to seal them from the outside. The wax and a liberal amount of vinegar were the preservatives of the day. No sodium benzoate, scorbic acid, or EDTA. Everything was natural. Yet, despite the totally natural preservatives, fifty was considered old age for most. The hard labors of life in this century overrode any benefit from an almost entirely natural and organic diet.

"Jonathan, Mister Grigsby said you should rub the tomatoes in your hair and any part of your body that was exposed to the skunk, then leave it sit for a good quarter of an hour before you bathe. He assures me that this will get rid of the odor," Dorcas explained.

"What about the lavender?" I asked. I hoped that the tomatoes would take its place.

"The lavender is for after the tomatoes, silly," Dorcas teased. "You don't want to reek of tomatoes and vinegar, do you?"

"Lavender it is," I replied. "*Lavender… I will end up smelling like a whore's bath in the Far East,*" again thinking to myself.

*   *   *   *   *

Bethany was entering her final night in the sweat lodge. By morning, she would have a plan to deal with Jonathan's imminent marriage. She already knew that the plan would not involve accepting Dorcas as a *fait accompli.*

Aiyana visited again just before nightfall, this time without any food; Bethany had eaten her last meal at midday and would not eat again until her time in the lodge was done. As the two women sat naked on bearskin rugs, they stared into the fire for several minutes before either of them spoke.

"Bethany, you seem relieved this evening. Do you have a plan?" Aiyana asked.

"Yes, I think I do. It will involve both you and Nechochwen," Bethany explained.

"So you are going to take Nechochwen as a husband?" Aiyana said, jumping ahead to a subject that Bethany was not yet ready to talk about.

"On that matter, I am undecided," Bethany declared. "He is suitable, but so much younger than me. He would have to understand that I am no longer able to produce children."

"Nechochwen has been alone for so long that I do not think he is suited to fatherhood," Aiyana offered. "I am sure he has already told you that the whites think he prefers the company of men, the type of company that is forbidden in the Bible," Aiyana explained.

This was not the first time Bethany had heard allegations that her would-be husband might be queer; the first came directly from Nechochwen himself. She tried not to believe it as fact. If her plan for Jonathan, whatever that turned out to be, was successful, Nechochwen would be left behind in 1658 when she jumped back to the 21st Century.

"When we have gone to the fishing village, I do not think that Jonathan has recognized me," Bethany said calmly. "Revealing myself to him will come as a surprise."

"You will certainly get the townspeople talking when you do that," Aiyana said, stifling a giggle.

Bethany had noticed how worldly and mature the stunningly beautiful Aiyana was in spite of her short "eighteen summers" of life. The whole situation – and their relationship – really was rather bizarre. Had it not been for that chance meeting at the circle carving, Bethany wondered if her present situation might have been completely different. In the silence of the sweat lodge, a thought suddenly came to Bethany: *If I were to take anyone other than Jonathan back with me to my time, it would be Aiyana.*

Bethany put the thought of Aiyana aside for the moment. She was suddenly very tired and needed to sleep.

264

The lodge had served its purpose: after two sleepless nights, her exhaustion would make it possible to sleep dreamlessly through the final night.

"Aiyana, I would like to sleep now," Bethany said softly.

"Yes, that would be wise," Aiyana said as she dressed to leave. "I will come for you in the morning, and you can tell Grandmother Chepi about your visions and the plan you have made."

At the entrance to the lodge, the still-naked Bethany took both of Aiyana's hands in hers and looked deeply into her eyes. They were as black as anthracite and sparkled in the glow from the fire. Words usually came easily to Bethany, but they suddenly escaped her. With a tender pat of her right hand, Bethany simply said, "Go…" Nothing else needed to be said.

Banking the fire for the night, Bethany curled up on the bearskin rug. For the first time since she had self-exiled in the sweat lodge, she pulled the bearskin over her and fell instantly asleep. No dreams plagued her as she slept, not even the one with JD on the opposite bank of the raging river.

The next morning, Bethany awoke full of energy. She didn't remember having this much energy since the last month of her pregnancy with JD. *"It certainly isn't a nesting instinct,"* she thought with an internal chuckle. *"I haven't done anything since I arrived, other than stalking Jonathan and worrying about JD. Those two things should have sapped all of my strength."*

Chapter Twenty-Six: Four Days Left
June 27 to July 1, 1658

Bethany's time in the sweat lodge was complete and she knew that Aiyana would arrive mid-day with fresh clothing. It was also time to allow the fire that she had kept burning for three whole days to die out. Her mind was made up: she could not let the wedding proceed and she now had a plan. *"It was elaborate, but yes, it would work,"* she told herself.

As if on cue, Aiyana came into the lodge.

"Bethany, I brought you new deerskin breeches and a blouse. You will need to look your best in the coming days."

Bethany squealed with delight at the new clothing. She had alternated between woven English fabric and deerskin since her arrival, only wearing the woven clothing while in the Quinnipiac village. She had developed a preference for the smoothness of the deerskin: it was so much more comfortable than the coarse hand-woven cloth.

Putting on the new attire, Bethany spoke to Aiyana. "We must tell the Grandmother of my plans."

"She is waiting for you," Aiyana replied. "But first we must make the lodge ready for the other women to use. I know one is close to 'her time' and she cannot be among the rest of us then."

With Bethany dressed, the two women spent the next hour returning the lodge to its "women's lodge" state. The hides were removed and the fire circle cleared of all debris. The dirt floor was swept and the cat trench latrine filled. Bethany hoped it would not smell too badly.

Walking out into the sunshine for the first time in three days, Bethany squinted against the bright glare. The sun felt amazing against her exposed skin, and the air was fresh without the aroma of woodsmoke, an aroma that permeated everything after her time in the lodge. She needed to bathe.

"Aiyana, will you take me to the river to bathe before our meal with Grandmother Chepi?" Bethany asked. "I stink of woodsmoke after being in the lodge for so long."

"We can go where I go. It is a nice cove with a waterfall. The water might be cold, but it will be clean and clear," Aiyana explained. "We can pick some mint leaves along the way to rub into our skin and hair."

As they walked to Aiyana's waterfall, Bethany was mostly silent and did not divulge any information about her plan. She was saving that for Grandmother Chepi. Aiyana, however, talked almost non-stop. Bethany found the young woman's voice soothing and did not want to interrupt her.

The two women played in the water as they swam and bathed; their giggles and squeals could be heard above the rush of the waterfall. It was like the two had become sisters, even with the thirty years' difference in their age. The situation reminded Bethany of her own childhood, playing in the pool with the neighbor children, and wishing that she had a brother or sister.

"Bethany, will you allow me to wash your hair?" Aiyana asked.

"Yes, you may," Bethany replied.

Kneeling on the sandy bottom of the stream, Bethany managed to keep most of her body underwater, out of prying eyes. Aiyana, on the other hand, was less modest and stood behind her, submerged only to the waist. Using the mint leaves and handfuls of sand, Aiyana tenderly washed Bethany's hair.

Eventually, Aiyana, too, knelt on the sand. She was behind Bethany, so close that Bethany could feel the young woman's breasts against her back and Aiyana's breath against the nape of her neck.

"What's happening here?" Bethany wondered, just as Aiyana's hands caressed her shoulders. It was an amazing feeling, unlike the touch of any man. She shivered as Aiyana's hands moved down her arms; Bethany also sensed that Aiyana was pressing more firmly against her back.

Bethany was completely lost in the moment and startled when Aiyana suddenly pulled away, breaking all physical contact.

"Finished. You should go under the water to rinse out the sand and mint leaves," Aiyana instructed Bethany.

*   *   *   *   *

The tomato bath seemed to have worked. I no longer reeked of skunk. That smell, though odiferous to all, was almost preferable to the smell of lavender. *"No self-respecting male naval officer would ever show up for work smelling of that stuff,"* I reminded myself. Dorcas, though, thought I smelled fresh and clean. Oh, the things we do for love!

We spent most of our day mending the few nets that had been left with us since the weekend. Nothing too strenuous, as it was normal wear and tear, not from heavy loads of fish that usually came ashore.

"Jonathan, darling, put your hand right here," Dorcas beamed, pointing at the bump that would become our child.

I put my hand on her belly and she placed her hand over mine.

"Can you feel that?" she squealed.

"Feel what?" I asked.

"It should feel like a little bird fluttering inside a sack," Dorcas explained.

"I don't feel anything at all," I said, my expression showing curiosity.

"I think it is our baby moving inside me," Dorcas said.

I knew that if anyone had seen our tender exchange, they would immediately suspect that Dorcas was in the family way. I also knew that if the information were in the wrong hands, it would be all over town before dinner – and there would be consequences for either or both of us. It was unlikely that Dorcas, being with child, would be subjected to another whipping. Me, on the other hand, well… I could be put into prison for as long as three months, the penalty prescribed by the English Parliament eight years earlier. The Puritan culture of the Colonies differed with England only on religion; civil law was another matter entirely. We had to be more discrete.

"Dorcas, my dear, after we are married, I will gladly spend more time feeling our child move inside you. Right now, though, it might give away that you are with child. We've kept it secret from everyone but Reverend and Goody MacKendrie and I think we should keep it that way."

"But Jonathan, people *will* count the number of months between our wedding day and the birth of our child. I'm already over four months gone, by my reckoning, and anything less than eight months will have people talking," Dorcas explained, "especially if it is a healthy baby."

"I'd never thought of it that way," I said, pursing my lips and nodding in agreement.

"I hope that the deacons will not take a strict view of our situation, with us both having been married before," Dorcas said calmly. "There are laws against fornication and the punishment could be quite severe."

"I certainly don't want to be sent to prison just because of an indiscretion –"

"An indiscretion?" Dorcas interrupted. "Is that what we are calling it now, Mister Harris? I thought it was anything but an indiscretion with all of the planning we have to put into being together when we are not here mending these smelly nets…" She burst into tears as she finished her diatribe.

Instead of engaging, I chose the silent option. Arguing with a pregnant woman was always a losing proposition for the man, or so I had heard from my Navy colleagues. I was the only one among my team who had not fathered multiple children, so I had to live vicariously through their experiences. I always knew when a new baby was on the way: the colleague spent an inordinate amount of time cleaning weapons or working out, anything to delay returning home.

My observations also noticed that the wives in most cases had become self-sufficient during the long absences of their husbands for missions abroad. In domestic settings, the husbands were more in the way than anything else. The only thing that kept some of these couples together was what transpired in the bedroom – usually resulting in a pregnancy whenever the husband was home for more than a month.

The females under my command in Special Warfare were a different breed entirely. Most remained unmarried and childless by choice, choosing to focus entirely on their careers without domestic distractions. To a woman, they were all driven and just as capable as the male warriors, some even more so because they felt they had something to prove. Most didn't simply accept the fact that they had already proven themselves by their selection as Special Warfare operators; rather, that they felt under continual scrutiny from male equals and superiors just waiting for them to screw up or let their guard down.

Why was I reminiscing about my time in the Navy? Here I was with a woman who loved me, who was pregnant with my child, who barely left my side – and I was reflecting back on my career. Was I going to regret my decision to marry Dorcas?

*   *   *   *   *

Back in the Quinnipiac village, Bethany was preparing to tell Chepi of her plan. She needed both Aiyana and Nechochwen to be there; they were both an integral part of her scheme. She was not completely sure that it would work and needed Chepi's alleged second sight.

Bethany entered Chepi's lodge with Aiyana and Nechochwen following closely behind. The old woman beckoned them to sit with her around the small but comforting fire. Bethany took her place between the other two; the seating arrangement was not lost on Chepi.

"Grandmother Chepi, I thank you for giving the time alone in the sweat lodge," Bethany began. "I have decided my way forward."

"Yes, child, please tell me," Chepi prompted.

"Jonathan is to be married on Monday, the day after the third reading of the banns in church," Bethany explained. "I must stop the ceremony even before Reverend MacKendrie guides them through the recitation of their vows."

Aiyana and Nechochwen were both looking intently at their friend. They knew they were to be part of the plan but had no idea what Bethany had in mind. They were not usually welcome in the white settler's church, instead holding services in their village whenever Reverend MacKendrie chose to visit – which was infrequently.

Bethany continued, "Once the ceremony is stopped, I will need two horses ready to ride away as quickly as possible. There will certainly be an outcry from the villagers, as I am sure several of them will recognize me from when the mob tried to rescue me last week."

"What do you want from my granddaughter and Nechochwen?" Chepi asked.

Bethany lowered her voice to a volume barely above a whisper. "They will slow down anyone who tries to follow. I must be safely hiding in the forest until nightfall before going to the circle tree, I do not expect Jonathan to come along quietly, so I will need Nechochwen to tie him up and lift him into the saddle."

"Your plan so far is admirable, child, but I fear there will be troubles along the way," Chepi replied.

"Grandmother," Aiyana interrupted, "is your second sight giving you any vision of what may happen?"

"No, Granddaughter, nothing clear but I do sense some kind of trouble."

Bethany leaned into the circle, made eye contact with the other three, and lowered her voice even more. "Here's how I plan to stop the wedding…"

Chapter Twenty-Seven: *Lacta Alea Est*
June 30 – July 1, 1658

As I sat with Dorcas in church on Sunday morning, I was strangely reminded of Julius Caesar crossing the Rubicon in 49 BCE. There was no turning back. The die was cast. *Lacta Alia Est.* It was a lesson in military history and strategy that was taught to all freshmen in the service academies. It certainly applied to my current situation.

Dorcas and I would, barring any intervention with the third and final reading of the banns today, be married tomorrow. Reverend MacKendrie, seemingly guided by the Almighty and given a sense of prescience, spoke about marriage in his sermon. Reading Proverbs 18:22, "*Whoso findeth a wife findeth a good thing, and obtaineth favor of the Lord,.*" MacKendrie acknowledged my arrival in New Haven as a castaway some three years earlier, Dorcas's trials and tribulations as an accused gossip and confirmed widow, and how our paths came together to bring us both love.

As MacKendrie spoke, Dorcas patted me tenderly on the back of my hand; all I could do was smile. I did sneak a furtive glance at her expanding waistline, knowing that it would not be much longer before her condition became quite obvious and unconcealable – even with the voluminous attire of the day. I had to revert my attention to the pulpit or I could have easily found myself staring at the wonder growing inside her.

In his sermon, MacKendrie made no mention of chastity before marriage. He knew full well that Dorcas was with child; it would have violated my trust for him to have spoken about it in his sermon. As with most emergent Protestant faiths, there was no requirement for a private confession through a priest; it was a precept of the so-called Free Church that the faithful confess their sins directly to God. Confession had even become part of Anglican and Protestant liturgies without the inherently Catholic trappings of the private confessional cubicle.

"Wait a minute," I thought to myself. *"I've never been a particularly religious person and yet I have this innate understanding of the differences between Catholicism and Protestantism. I must have been paying attention in school after all!"*

I brought my attention back to MacKendrie's closing remarks. "In the Bible, Ruth said 'whither thou goest, I will go; and where thou lodgest, I will lodge: thy people shall be my people and thy God my God.' This is what it means to be married. To follow one another to the ends of the earth, through sickness and in health, for richer for poorer, in the good times and the bad. In Jesus' name, Amen."

MacKendrie descended the two steps from the elevated platform that served as the pulpit. He stopped and bowed his head in a short prayer, then turned to face the congregation. Giving a quick nod to Dorcas and me, he began with the third reading of our banns:

"I read the banns of marriage between Mister Jonathan Harris and the widow Dorcas Parham Pinkerton, both of Newhaven. This is the third reading of the banns. If any of you know cause or just impediment why these two persons are not to be joined together in Holy Matrimony, you are to declare it forthwith."

It seemed as if the entire congregation was expecting someone to come out of the woodwork and announce an impediment to our imminent marriage. Men and women alike looked to the rear door, then at each other. I was an outsider, and no one other than Captain Palmer, Dorcas Parham Pinkerton or Fatou the slave-healer knew many details about my travails at sea. I had been circumspect about who I shared any of those details with, deciding early that the fewer details known about my escapades, the better it would be for me.

Meanwhile, the women of the village considered Dorcas to be nothing more than a harlot and Captain Tettersell was the only person who might have derogatory information on the Parham family. It was a complicated situation that could have been made even worse by a malicious turn of phrase in response to MacKendrie's final reading of the banns. Thankfully, aside from the low murmuring at the end of the banns, nothing untoward happened.

*   *   *   *   *

In the Quinnipiac village about five miles away, Bethany was a nervous wreck. She had put her plan in place, made sure that Aiyana and Nechochwen would support her, and was now simply counting the hours until the wedding ceremony would begin. It likely would be a long and mostly sleepless night.

Her thoughts also turned to JD, Jonathan's son, and how he was doing in the care of Maria and Pierre. Bethany's disappearance had been anything but planned; she presumed JD was in good hands but was not entirely sure. Yes, Pierre Delacroix was tolerant, if not affectionate, towards the child, and JD certainly responded well to

Pierre's attention – but there was something that bothered her about the arrangement.

Maria, on the other hand, loved JD like he was her own son and Bethany was not even slightly worried. Besides, she had signed a legal document giving Maria power of attorney *in loco parentis* not long before they set out for New Haven a couple of months earlier. In Bethany's absence, Maria had parental control, custody, and responsibility for JD's needs.

Late in the afternoon, Reverend MacKendrie arrived to conduct services for the Quinnipiac believers. Bethany always attended when MacKendrie visited, as she found the gatherings to be of comfort. Chepi, too, was a regular attendee and where Chepi went, so did most of the rest of the band. When preaching to the Quinnipiacs, MacKendrie's sermons always seemed to have a missionary theme to them, as if he were still trying to justify their conversion to the faith.

Because a few of the Quinnipiacs had not mastered the English language, it usually fell to Aiyana to interpret. She had acquired the language as a child and was nearly bilingual, There were very few concepts that she could not translate into the Quinnipiac tongue. That small group, elders like Chepi, usually sat to the rear of the group so that Aiyana's voice would not distract the rest of the worshippers.

Usually, Bethany sat in rapt attention, her gaze fixed hypnotically on the Reverend. Today was different. She averted her eyes to avoid contact with his, as if she had something to hide, perhaps embarrassing to both her and to the Quinnipiacs. If MacKendrie had been more in tune with his congregation than his own ego, he might have noticed something was amiss. He still did not recognize that Bethany was a white woman, so he did not go out of his way to engage with her as he would have a settler woman on Sunday morning.

After the service, it was customary for Reverend MacKendrie and his wife, Penelope, to remain in with the Quinnipiacs for the evening meal. This Sunday was no exception, in spite of the wedding scheduled for the next day. Conversation was usually stilted, as the lifestyles of the settlers and natives were so radically different. Still trying to stay *incognito* as a Quinnipiac, she took the bold step of asking MacKendrie a direct question.

"Reverend MacKendrie, isn't the town preparing for a wedding tomorrow?" Bethany asked. "I see that Mister Harris is to be the groom."

"Indeed, he is," MacKendrie replied. "He came to us about three years ago as a rescued castaway and has been a fine addition to the village. He and the Widow Pinkerton will make a fine couple." It didn't register with MacKendrie to ascertain how Bethany knew about the wedding and the bridegroom.

Bethany stifled a laugh following his reply. Even from her distant observations with the spyglass, she had surmised that Dorcas Parham Pinkerton was already with child and that their marriage was necessary to preclude the child's status as a bastard. Colonial law was pretty clear on that subject and the child would be marked for life if not born to married parents, regardless of the interval between the wedding and birth.

Bethany found the engagement with the MacKendries to be tedious and the conversation forced. It felt as if the Reverend and his wife were trying to prove how good they were. Not wishing to remain in such a situation, she feigned a headache and took her leave of the gathering. As Bethany expected, Aiyana followed her to their lodge.

"Aiyana, I hope I am ready to do what must be done," said Bethany; she sounded worried.

"Just follow your plan and your heart and all will be well," Aiyana replied.

"We will need to be in town, hiding in the woods just outside the church, a little before the clock strikes noon." Bethany said as she started to recap her plan to Aiyana.

"We've discussed this many times, Bethany. I know what to do. Nechochwen knows what to do. Grandmother Chepi will do her part as well," Aiyana reminded her.

*　　*　　*　　*　　*

As I walked around the village green just after sunset, I observed Reverend MacKendrie and his wife returning home in their wagon. I wondered how they had managed to navigate in the dark on a moonless night; it must have been that their horse knew the way. Unlike my experiences in the 21st Century with night vision goggles and GPS support, travelers relied on their horses' innate abilities to always return to their home barn. The MacKendrie's horse was no different.

My concern at this late hour was that Dorcas's wedding dress would not be ready in time for the ceremony tomorrow at noon. Goody MacKendrie and Fatou were supposed to work together on the final fitting. They alone would be allowed to see Dorcas's expanding waistline and adjust the dress accordingly. Other women had volunteered, more out of curiosity than anything else, but were politely declined. Dorcas knew what was at stake.

We had also agreed to hold with tradition, that I would not see Dorcas until she walked down the aisle on our wedding day. I knew this tradition applied largely to arranged marriages; ours was anything but arranged, and the more we kept to tradition, the less likely it was that we would deal with gossiping backlash later.

Fatou had apparently been watching for the MacKendries to return as well. Within minutes of the Reverend unharnessing the two-horse team, Fatou strode purposefully across the green to the parsonage adjacent to the church. She carried her bag, which I knew contained a sewing kit in addition to her healer's equipment. Knocking on the door of the MacKendrie residence, Fatou was ushered quickly inside. In the brief period the door was ajar, I could clearly see Dorcas standing inside the front vestibule. She looked radiant, even from afar. I hoped that my brief glimpse of her was not going to curse our wedding day.

As I sat outside my cottage taking in the evening air, Captains Palmer and Tettersell approached from the southeast corner of the green. They stopped to speak with me; I could tell they had been drinking.

"Mister Harris, you are getting married tomorrow!" Palmer exclaimed. I could tell he had been drinking.

Tettersell added to the conversation, "Won't you join us for a libation to celebrate the imminent occasion?"

"Gentlemen, I do not wish to venture into God's house tomorrow with a throbbing head reminding me of the night before," I responded, surprising even myself at the sudden outburst of piety. "But... I will accompany you to the tavern for one... and only one... draught of ale."

"Good, good!" Palmer exclaimed, winking at Tettersell as he slapped me convivially on the back.

Three hours later, the two captains walked me back to my cottage. I had gone against my word and had more ale than I probably should have; it was an immediate trip to the privy to void my bladder. I was also afraid that I would lose the contents of my stomach in due course, so when I returned to my cottage, I placed an oaken bucket at the bedside. That preparation proved to be serendipitous.

Not long after sunrise, I heard a knock at my door. It was Fatou coming to me as a healer. She somehow knew that I would be hung over and was prepared with herbal concoctions to mitigate the crapulence caused by my excess the night before.

"Mister Harris, you must drink this potion in one gulp," Fatou instructed.

I had learned a long time ago that her instructions were best followed. She had brought both me and Dorcas back from the brink of eternal darkness and I trusted her completely. I took the pewter cup from her hands.

"Lord in Heaven, this whatever it is tastes awful! Fatou!" I exclaimed, sputtering and gagging as the potion slid down my throat. "What is it that I just drank?"

"Mister Harris, it is a potion of pork fat, dried red pepper, vinegar, and... the powder of dried bull bollocks," she explained.

Her description was fine until she got to the powdered bull's testicles. That brought about another round of retching and eventual emesis. "Fatou... that... was...

terrible…” I said through gags and expectorations. Funny thing, though: my hangover was instantly cured.

“See, Mister Harris? It worked,” Fatou said with a smile that was missing more than half of her teeth. “If it hadn’t the next remedy was to wash your private parts in vinegar.”

I decided right then and there that my hangover was cured. There was no way I was washing the family jewels in Puritan vinegar. I certainly didn’t want anything down there to be pickled on our wedding night!

My hangover now under control, Fatou bathed me as she had done aboard the “Desire,” using soap scented with strawberries. They had just come into season and the settlers had mastered their cultivation over the last two decades, thanks to the Natives. The strawberry-scented soap was preferable to the lavender that I detested.

Now cleanly washed, Fatou took her leave and was replaced by Captain Palmer. It was now his responsibility to ensure that I was appropriately attired and that I would arrive at the church on time. It was another tradition intended to keep the groom from bolting and disappearing into the forests to avoid the commitment of marriage. I certainly had no intention of abandoning my betrothal, so it was largely a symbolic presence.

Chapter Twenty-Eight: A Summer's Day
July 1, 1658

I was too nervous (and hung over) to eat. Even so, Fatou had left about a dozen fresh-baked rolls behind in case I decided to eat before heading to the church. After her bovine testicular concoction, I had lost all of my appetite, and the rolls sat on the plate with Captain Palmer salivating over them. I had to admit that they did smell quite delectable.

As I looked out my front window, I saw a carriage pulling up outside of Dorcas's cottage. It was driven by the liveryman, decked out in his best black attire. Alighting from the carriage was none other than Captain Tettersell, the very man that Dorcas had avoided ever since she knew he was in New Haven. I was puzzled and would ask Dorcas about Tettersell's presence after the ceremony.

Captain Palmer checked his German-made pocket watch repeatedly. I wasn't sure if it was an affectation designed to show off his wealth or if he was truly keeping track of the time. Either way, I knew I would not be late for my own wedding. I was ready and hoped that Dorcas shared my enthusiasm.

At about eleven, Palmer insisted that I dress for the ceremony. It was more time than I needed, aside from tying the 17th Century cravat, which continued to challenge my dexterity. Thankfully, Captain Palmer was able to assist, and I sat ready, quite the dapper gentleman, to meet my bride in less than an hour.

*　　*　　*　　*　　*

Nechochwen had four horses bridled and ready to tie up in the woods outside the church; the fourth horse was for Jonathan Harris as Bethany had planned. Aiyana was dressed in her best and newest deerskin clothing and moccasins. Bethany, on the other hand, had decided that her plan would be most effective if she were in more traditional Puritan attire that would allow Jonathan to recognize her instantly.

Concerned that everything could go awry and a hasty escape become necessary, Bethany decided to carry a complete deerskin ensemble with her to New Haven, leaving it behind with Nechochwen and the horses while she and Aiyana went to the church.

Taking into consideration the distance from the Quinnipiac village, Chepi urged the trio to begin their journey. She instinctively knew that this likely was the last time that she would be seeing Bethany and embraced her in a tearful farewell, the physical display of affection quite out of character for Chepi. In just a few short weeks, the two women had grown to love each other almost as if they were sisters. It was a poignant moment for both of them.

On their way to the church, Bethany did not speak. As was her nature, she was playing every possible scenario in her mind. Would her plan work? Could she make it to the circle tree before Dorcas and the townspeople knew what was happening? Would anyone believe her? She was on the verge of an anxiety attack by the time they had gone a mile from the Quinnipiac village.

"Bethany, you are more skittish than a doe during the rut," Aiyana teased. "You should just close your eyes and breathe deeply, remembering your time in the sweat lodge."

"I am trying to do just that," Bethany responded, "but my mind is racing and I don't have answers for many of my questions. The plan could still fail."

"Put that thought out of your mind," Aiyana commanded. "You need to have your wits about you and not be distracted by what might or might not happen."

Nechochwen was riding a few strides to the read and could only smile. *"I never will understand women,"* he thought to himself. Still, he wanted Bethany for his wife, and hoped against hope that her plan would fail.

The trio paused in an area where they could not be easily seen from the churchyard but where they could observe the comings and goings. All three dismounted and Nechochwen put the horses on a quick-release picket line. From their concealed location, they saw a carriage pulling up to the church. The ceremony was about to begin. Time was of the utmost importance as Puritan wedding ceremonies were ridiculously short.

*   *   *   *   *

I had been standing at the front of the church with Reverend MacKendrie and Captain Palmer for about fifteen minutes when we heard the carriage pull up outside. I couldn't wait to see Dorcas in her wedding dress as she walked down the aisle. The church doors opened and the first person to enter from the carriage was Goody MacKendrie. She was the 17th Century equivalent of the Matron of Honor.

Puritan worship, including wedding ceremonies, were devoid of any music except for chanted psalms. As

Penelope MacKendrie strode slowly up the aisle, the congregation chanted the first five verses of Psalm 128:

"Blessed is everyone that feareth the Lord; that walketh in his ways.

For thou shalt eat the labour of thine hands; happy shalt thou be, and it shall be well with thee.

Thy wife shall be as a fruitful vine by the sides of thine house; thy children like olive plants around thy table.

Behold, that thus shall the man be blessed that feareth the Lord.

The Lord shall bless thee out of Zion; and thou shalt see the good of Jerusalem all the days of thy life."

I knew exactly why Reverend MacKendrie had chosen this particular psalm for the service. It was the third verse, wishing the fruitfulness of children on our marriage. I stifled a chuckle when the congregation hit that verse; it would soon be obvious to everyone that yes, indeed, we would be fruitful!

Once Penelope MacKendrie reached the front of the church, her husband signaled the congregation to rise. The doors opened and Dorcas entered, on the arm of none other than Captain Tettersell. I knew she despised the man, but I had an epiphany that he was probably the closest thing she had to a living relative with her parents both already deceased. Fatou entered right behind them and closed the doors, remaining respectfully at the rear of the church.

"She is absolutely beautiful," I whispered to myself. Her dress was a lavender satin, imported from France. Fatou and Goody MacKendrie had done a wonderful job of tailoring it to conceal Dorcas's pregnancy; the addition of a bustle of sorts accentuated her hips and drew attention away from her midsection.

Modesty, of course, was appropriate and the dress completely covered any decolletage. Fatou had added a little lace for ornamentation in that area, which also drew curious eyes upward. She was the most beautiful woman I had seen in New Haven since my arrival. *"Reverend MacKendrie, can we just get on with it?"* I mused silently.

When Dorcas reached the front of the church, Captain Tettersell placed her hand in mine, bowed from the neck, and returned to the front bench. With Dorcas facing me for the moment, my eyes met hers and we both smiled. I even felt myself tearing up a little bit.

Turning to face the good Reverend, he nodded to both of us and smiled. Being a Free Church pastor, he took a little liberty with the ceremony, first choosing to read from the New Testament, Paul's Epistle to the Ephesians, Chapter Five: "*Husbands, love your wives, even as Christ loved the church, and gave himself for it...*"

At the end of the reading, MacKendrie paused, gathered his thoughts and bellowed, "Once again, I ask: Is there any among you who have cause that this man and this woman should not be joined together in holy matrimony? I command you to speak now or forever hold your peace."

Once more, I looked at Dorcas and smiled as the congregation stirred and squirmed in their seats. There had been no objections when the banns had been read and I did not expect anything to happen now.

The entire congregation visibly jumped in surprise when there were three sudden and very loud knocks on the church door. Husbands looked at their wives. I looked at Dorcas. MacKendrie, too, was puzzled. Nobody knew what was going on. Were we under attack? Pirates? Highwaymen?

Fatou, being the closest person to the door, opened it. Standing in the doorway was a woman dressed in a plain cotton dress, her face covered with a matching linen mask. The congregation gasped in unison, wondering what was to happen next.

I watched as the woman walked up the aisle to the front pew. There, she said in a loud voice, "I have cause for this marriage not to take place."

I thought I recognized the voice. Something stirred deep inside my brain and in my heart.

"Good Woman," MacKendrie bellowed indignantly, "you are in the House of the Lord and I ask… no, I demand that you remove your face covering and identify yourself. I trust you have reason to disrupt this ceremony."

Slowly, the woman lifted the mask, starting at the chin. As she raised the mask, she said, "This man has fathered a child. A legitimate child. Not a bastard." Again, the congregation gasped, more loudly than the first time.

The mask was now up to her nose.

"Could it be…? No… It can't be…" I was trying to convince myself that what I was seeing was just a figment of my imagination.

Completely removing the mask, she spoke once more. "Jonathan Harris is married to me. I am his wife, Bethany. He has been missing for some time. On our last night together before he disappeared, he left me in the family way."

"Woman, we will have no such talk in this church!" MacKendrie bellowed again.

My heart raced. Sweat began to bead on my forehead. My palms became as slippery as an eel. My face flushed, followed by a wave of dizziness and nausea. I felt very unwell, as if the full weight of a wine cask was on my chest.

My voice came in choking gasps. "Bethany? Is that you? How did you – "

*　*　*　*　*

Before Jonathan Harris could complete the sentence, he collapsed to the floor, gasping for breath. Seeing her betrothed in such a state, Dorcas screamed in panic, then went into hysteria. Her screams, moans, and cries were visceral and unnerving.

The village physician, Doctor Montague, ran to Jonathan's aid, as did Fatou all the way from the rear of the church. By the time they got to Jonathan's prostrate form, his eyes were unseeing in the stare of death.

Bethany stood there trying to understand what was happening. *"Was it too much for Jonathan to take in all at once?"* she wondered.

As Montague and Fatou examined Jonathan, all eyes of the congregation were on them. Bethany used the distraction to edge her way back towards the church door, ready to break into a run if necessary. She had not planned for this turn of events and was, as they said in her time, "winging it."

Montague looked up at Reverend MacKendrie and shook his head. "He's dead," the doctor said in a very quiet voice, gently closing Jonathan's eyes. Fatou produced a linen cloth from her own bag and covered Jonathan's face. Reverend MacKendrie knelt next to the body and made the sign of the cross.

From somewhere in the church, a woman bellowed, "Witch!" Another voice hollered, "Arrest her!" Another shouted, "Murderer!"

Other congregants joined the cry and before long the entire group was buzzing with the accusation that Bethany was a witch. A mob scene was developing. It wouldn't be long before the situation devolved into pandemonium

Bethany had eased her way almost to the rear of the church before the first accusatory cry. As the clamor rose, she turned on her heels, gathered her dress up to her waist and broke into a run. Fortunate for Bethany, the village constable was seated in the middle of the second pew from the front and could not give immediate chase without pushing at least thirty people out of his way.

Turning left onto the forest path, Bethany quickly met up with Nechochwen, Aiyana, and the horses. Time was of the essence if they were all to escape. The two Quinnipiacs saw the urgency in Bethany's expression, helped Bethany mount her horse and then mounted their own in one fluid motion. No words were exchanged until they were out of sight of the church and deep into the forest.

Slowing the horses to a quick walk, Aiyana pulled alongside Bethany, dodging overhanging branches as she did so.

"Bethany, what happed in the church?" Aiyana asked.

"Jonathan is dead. His heart must have stopped when I presented myself as his wife and declared that we had a son," Bethany responded. "I had not planned for that…"

Nechochwen, on the lead horse, stopped and turned around so that he could speak. "I heard the cries of 'witch!' coming from the church. Did you cast a spell on Jonathan?"

Bethany giggled nervously, then told him, "There is no such thing as a witch, Nechochwen. People will call others a witch when they can't explain something that happened – like Jonathan dying suddenly. I didn't do anything to cause that other than showing myself. That caused his heart to stop beating."

"We must tell Grandmother Chepi," Nechochwen replied.

"Yes, that would be wise," Bethany agreed.

Chapter Twenty-Nine: Departure
Afternoon and Evening of July 1, 1658

Once in the Quinnipiac village, Aiyana and I dismounted and handed the reins to Nechochwen, who would take care of the horses. I was glad when Aiyana gently took my arm to support me, as the events of the last hour had left me unsteady on my feet. We strode across the village and entered Chepi's lodge.

"Child, what happened at the church?" Chepi asked.

"Grandmother, I did everything as I had planned. I went into the church and told everyone, before God, that I was Jonathan's wife and that we shared a child. Before he could say more than a few words, he dropped dead on the floor."

With the fight-or-flight adrenaline rush wearing off, I suddenly realized the precarity of my situation. Dropping to my knees in the soft dirt next to Chepi's fire, I began to sob inconsolably. Aiyana quickly knelt beside me and wrapped her arms around me in comfort.

"Were you followed?" Chepi asked.

Nechochwen answered, "We were well out of sight before anyone else came out of the church. They might believe Bethany vanished into the air like a spirit. I don't think they heard our horses, either."

"Child, you must go to the circle tonight and try to return to your own time. There is no moon, so the circle will be ready for you," Chepi explained. "My granddaughter may go with you to the circle to bid her goodbye. You can leave once it is fully dark."

"Grandmother Chepi, I was not expecting any of this to happen. I thought that Jonathan would be here with me and that we would be going back to our time together." I was still reeling from the stark reality of now being totally alone (unless, of course, I counted Pierre Delacroix and Maria). *How am I going to deal with all of this back in 2018?"* I pondered. I was truly saddened by the fact that I would be leaving these people who I had come to love as my own family.

"Bethany, you must eat something before your journey," Aiyana pleaded. "One of the men has just returned from the river with a few wonderful fish."

"I would like that very much," I said. I suddenly realized that I was more than a little hungry; I hadn't eaten anything since we left for the church that morning.

With Nechochwen and Aiyana on either side of me and Chepi directly across the fire from me, we ate. The fish was some of the best I had ever eaten and the fresh vegetables from the spring garden were perfectly cooked. *"Much better than 21st Century processed stuff,"* I thought.

Sitting there, I felt perfectly at home and integrated into the Quinnipiac culture. I also knew that I likely would be one of the last white people to share their lifestyle before the tribe all but disappeared or was absorbed into other tribes. Knowing what lay in store for their lineage, I asked Grandmother Chepi to tell me the stories of her ancestors, making sure that I committed everything she was telling me to memory. I knew that I might not be able to rewrite history in my time, but Chepi knowing that her knowledge was safe for the future was the best gift of thanks I could possibly give her.

For the next two or three hours while we waited for nightfall, Chepi recounted how her ancestors, the "People of the Long Water Land," lived and died. With tears in her eyes, she recounted the smallpox epidemic of 1634 and 1635 and how many of her people had died. "It was right after the settlers came in their ships," Chepi explained as a cause-and-effect story. She continued with the stories of how, "just twenty summers earlier," the white settlers began taking over Quinnipiac territory and pushing her people west.

Her voice suddenly went silent as she cocked her head to identify a far-away sound. Chepi looked Aiyana in the eye and said simply, "It's time."

"Come, Bethany, we must leave now." The urgency in Aiyana's voice was sufficient to hasten my departure.

Stepping outside of Chepi's lodge, I immediately understood why I had to leave. In the distance, I could see the light of about a dozen torches approaching from the northeast on the forest path between the Quinnipiac village and New Haven. The torch-bearing crowd was anything but silent: "We're coming for the witch" was all I needed to hear. Somehow, they had surmised my destination after Jonathan's unexpected demise.

"Aiyana, please take me to the circle tree," I pleaded.

"Yes, my friend, we must go," Aiyana answered.

As we left the comfort of Chepi's lodge, Aiyana stopped us at the edge of the forest, where we hid in the underbrush. "We need our eyes to be ready to see in the dark," she explained. Once our eyes adjusted, we would head in the direction of the circle tree, the place where my adventure into the 17th Century had started.

My vision quickly adjusted to the darkness. Though there was no moon, I could see well enough that I would avoid most of the hazards of the forest and was confident that I could make my way to our destination alone if necessary. Aiyana held me back, though, as the mob had just arrived at Chepi's lodge and were demanding I be turned over to them. If we left now, we would certainly be discovered and caught.

The mob railed against Chepi and the entire tribe. I could clearly hear some of the epithets that were being shouted. Brandishing their torches, the mob threatened to burn down every lodge, starting with Chepi's.

Suddenly, a shot rang out, and with a collective gasp, the mob fell silent.

Seconds after the crowd-stopping shot, Reverend MacKendrie rode into the Quinnipiac village on horseback, tucking a pistol into the belt of his tunic.

"Gentlemen and Ladies, in the name of God Almighty, you are to cease and desist. Grandmother Chepi is a God-fearing woman. I will ask her if the mysterious woman is in her village, and she will tell me the truth."

"This is it," I whispered to Aiyana. "If they don't believe the Reverend or your grandmother, blood will be spilled."

MacKendrie posed his question: "Chepi, a mystery woman appeared before us during the wedding and claimed to be Jonathan Harris's husband. Do you know where she is?"

"Reverend MacKendrie, I stand before you and God and tell you that I do not know where she is right now." Chepi sounded as if she were taking a witness oath in a TV drama. She was as solemn as I had ever seen her.

"Citizens, there you have it," MacKendrie cajoled. "The mystery woman's whereabouts are presently unknown."

"She's a witch and could have disappeared in thin air!" a man heckled from the middle of the crowd. Another hollered, "Why should we believe a heathen?"

"Silence!" MacKendrie bellowed with the authority of a drill sergeant. The mob obeyed.

Reverend MacKendrie knew he would have to prove to this mob that Chepi was indeed a Christian. "Chepi, have you been baptized into the Christian faith?"

"Yes, Reverend MacKendrie. By the good Reverend Eaton himself almost twenty summers ago," Chepi answered.

"Can you recite the Twenty-Third Psalm?"

Chepi knelt to the ground, folded her hands, raised her gaze to the heavens and began her recitation:

"The Lord is my shepherd: I shall not want.

He maketh me to lie down in green pastures; He leadeth me beside the still waters.

He restoreth my soul: He leadeth me in the paths of righteousness for His name's sake.

Yea, though I walk through the valley of the shadow of death, I will fear no evil – "

Reverend MacKendrie interrupted her. "You shall not fear evil today, good Chepi. You have proven to me that you are indeed a God-fearing Christian." He turned to the crowd before continuing, "I dare any one of you to challenge this woman's faith or her convictions."

The mob went completely silent. Men and women alike hung their heads in shame and avoided eye contact with Reverend MacKendrie. A few of the mob turned and began shuffling back to New Haven. He had defused a potentially dangerous and explosive situation.

"In the name of God, I command you to disperse from this evil pursuit. Return to your homes and pray to God Almighty for forgiveness this night!" It was MacKendrie's benediction of necessity.

Aiyana squeezed my hand once more. The danger had passed and we could be on our way. I knew that the circle tree, even in daylight was about a twenty-minute walk from the Quinnipiac village; at night it could take a few minutes longer. I would be home… back in the 21st Century… very soon.

"Bethany, we are safe now. We can remove ourselves from this hiding place," Aiyana said.

All the way to the circle tree, Aiyana held my hand tightly, interlacing her fingers with my own. She did not want to let go even when I relaxed my own grip. What sort of a message was she trying to send? I wondered.

We reached the circle tree in about half an hour. I stood there contemplating my next move and was torn between following Chepi's instructions or simply staying where I was. Jonathan was dead, so I had no reason to stay aside from my relationship with Chepi, Aiyana, Nechochwen and their people. Staying, I would have a husband and an extended family. Going back, I would return to my own son, JD, who I trusted had been in excellent care from Pierre and Maria. Selfishly, I thought about how JD would be my eternal reminder of my life with Jonathan Harris.

I loved my son and my mothering instincts were winning out over the strong desire to stay. Now sweating profusely, I took a step closer to the tree. Aiyana was behind me, less than an arm's length away.

My hand trembled as I first touched the top of the circle. As I slowly and purposefully traced the first 180 degrees of arc, clockwise from top to bottom dead center, I was at peace with my decision. My hand stopped trembling. A transcendent calm came over me and I thought I could feel the tree coming to life under my touch.

My trace of the circle once again reached the top and I placed my right hand in the center, as Chepi had instructed me. As I raised my left hand to shoulder height in preparation to place it over my right, Aiyana suddenly grabbed me around the waist, put her mouth next to my ear and whispered, "I am coming with you."

Those words were more compelling than any I had ever heard in my entire life and I smiled as I placed my left hand over my right. Before I could blink, Aiyana and I became one and we were on our way through time and space.

We moved slowly at first and I could clearly see events in history as they flashed by. The Salem Witch Trials… the American Revolution… Gettysburg…

As our speed increased, I saw San Juan Hill… the trenches of World War I… Pearl Harbor… Hiroshima… Neil Armstrong on the moon… Khe Sanh… Nixon's resignation… the Iranian revolution… the World Trade Center buildings collapsing… it was all a blur.

We slowed slightly as the timeline neared my own in 2018. I saw the improbable election of Donald Trump and his gloom-and-doom inaugural address… School shootings in Texas and Florida… Prince Harry and Megan Markle getting married…

Suddenly, as if we had hit a concrete wall, our forward progress stopped and everything went black. Dazed by our

Orwellian time travel, I felt my body to be sure I was still intact and discovered that Aiyana was still there with me and still holding tightly onto my waist.

As my awareness of time and place returned, I realized that I was once again naked – just like I was when I made the jump 360 years back in time. Aiyana, too, was naked. I surmised that clothing did not pass through the portal the same way as human flesh did.

Something about our surroundings seemed familiar. I had been here before. Our return point was not random.

Suddenly, a candle flickered to life in a sconce on the wall. Directly opposite that wall was a steep staircase. I knew immediately where I was: in the catacomb under the church where Reverend Mather had taken us on the day I jumped back to 1658.

"Aiyana, are you hurt?" I asked.

"No, Bethany. I am not. That was… I am without words to describe it," Aiyana said excitedly.

I looked to the staircase and saw that two track suits had been hung there. Was it by serendipity or by design that they were there? I would never know that answer. We certainly could not climb the stairs and emerge from under the altar in our birthday suits… On a small circular table at the bottom of the stairs was a key, which I immediately recognized as being a key to the door of my suite at the hotel. I would need to take it with me.

"I think we were meant to put those clothes on," I told Aiyana as I pointed towards the staircase.

"I know. It is the same thing that happens every time," Aiyana said, locking her gaze with my own.

"What happens every time?" I asked.

"Clothing," she said tersely.

"You mean… you've… done this before?"

"Yes, Bethany. Two other times. But unlike you, I cannot hop between times alone. I must travel with someone… I chose you."

"Me? Why me? Have there been others?" I asked, I was talking rapid-fire.

"Yes. Many others. But never more than one at a time. One must leave before another can arrive. There is always a gap between each visitor and we never know how long that gap will be. We are the ones who keep placing the documents that Reverend Mather adds to his collection."

Everything now made sense. Other time travelers were transporting documents across time and place, enabling insight on the past. No wonder Reverend Mather wanted to share his findings – and the underground chamber – with me and my team.

As I stood there listening to her story, I remembered how totally relaxed and comfortable I was with Aiyana, even when we were naked. In fact, I wanted nothing more than to pull her close and feel her flesh against my own. The desire to do so was consuming me, so much that I did not want to dress and climb that staircase. I had never before in my life experienced such intense feelings for a woman.

Aiyana sensed that something was troubling me. Keeping her eyes locked on mine, she took the few short steps across the underground chamber. Within an arm's reach, she extended her hands and took mine into her own.

"Is what I think is happening really happening?" I wondered.

I felt Aiyana gently pull me towards her. In another time, I might have resisted, but did not. As if in a trance, I took a step closer to Aiyana and wrapped my arms around her, pulling our naked bodies together. It felt so natural and so right… I didn't want this to end.

The next few minutes (or was it hours?) was a blur. I don't remember the specifics but I do remember being totally satisfied and at peace with myself. Whatever this "it" was, it was better than anything I had experienced with a man, not even with Jonathan.

As the fog of contentment lifted, I realized that we probably should dress and venture aboveground. As we dressed, I told Aiyana more about JD and a little about my relationship with Pierre.

"Is Pierre going to be your husband?" Aiyana asked.

"As a matter of fact, no. He is not the sort of man I could marry and be content with for the rest of my life," I answered. "Besides, I now have you…"

Chapter Thirty: Arrival
July 2, 2018

We reached the top of the staircase just after midnight on the morning of July 2, 2018. I was the first to crawl out from under the altar and relieved to see the brightly lit "EXIT" signs over each of the doorways. I was back in my own time. Electric lights. Indoor plumbing. Things I had taken for granted.

Aiyana followed, seeming to accept her new environment as normal; I had expected her to be awestruck. Once she was clear of the hidden compartment under the altar, I motioned for her to slide it closed on its tracks. It slid into place with a resounding "clunk" that echoed throughout the church.

"My temporary home is not far from here," I told Aiyana. "JD, Pierre, and Maria will be there."

"Bethany, don't you recognize this place, this church?" Aiyana queried.

Looking around for a few moments, I suddenly realized it was the church where I last saw Jonathan… where I told Jonathan that he already had a son… where Jonathan had dropped dead from the surprise of my arrival. Where I was accused of being a witch. I never wanted to set foot in this church again.

"Let's go," I beckoned. "I cannot stay here a moment longer." My tone meant business.

We walked quickly down the aisle and out the back door of the church. It was not alarmed, so we left unnoticed. A few minutes later, we were at the hotel where I had left JD, Maria, and my team.

Taking the elevator to my floor, Aiyana and I walked to the end of the hall and the door to my suite. I took the key from my pocket, inserted it in the lock, and opened the door. The suite was neat and tidy, just like I had kept it before my… whatever it was called… and I was impressed that it had remained that way. Maria was doing much more than just caring for JD.

Within a few seconds of entering, I heard voices coming from the direction of Maria's bedroom. A man's voice and a woman's voice. It was not the sound of normal conversation, and I could see from the gap at the bottom of the door that a light was on in the bedroom. Listening more closely, I recognized the voices of Maria and Pierre and knew that they weren't exactly exchanging bedtime stories.

Rather than walking to their room and entering unannounced, I quietly took Aiyana to JD's room. He was sound asleep, snoring a toddler's snore.

"He's beautiful!" Aiyana whispered.

"Yes, he is," I agreed. "In the morning, you can meet him properly."

Both exhausted, we headed for my bedroom. It was spotless, again just like I had left it. Even the ensuite bathroom sparkled. Aiyana pushed past me and into the bathroom, obviously no stranger to its fixtures or functions, and closed the door. A few moments later, I heard the sound of toilet paper being unrolled, followed by a flush.

"Hmm… there is so much more to this woman than I thought…" I said out loud.

Coming out of the bathroom, Aiyana smiled at me. She seemed to know what I was thinking. "We'll talk more about all of this in the morning," she said with a twinkle in her eye. "Right now, I am just too tired."

Pulling back the covers on the tightly made king bed, we undressed, laid down, and drew the covers over our bodies. The distance quickly closed between us, and I was once again in Aiyana's arms. With just enough light from the streetlight outside, I could see that she was smiling as she leaned forward to kiss me on the mouth. It certainly was not a peck-on-the-cheek of friendship, but a seductive, passionate lover's kiss – which I willingly and readily returned. Exhausted though we both professed to be, it was quite a while longer before we finally fell asleep.

Yes, tomorrow was going to be an interesting day!

Author's Note

This book, the ninth released in my "Lineage Series," is a departure from my usual *modus operandi*. It is still historical fiction, but less about the historical events as they are taking place and more about the people involved in the story. I also added a "time hop" dimension that brought the story to life.

Regardless, there are several intersections with my family tree and other historical events that are mentioned in the book. I will do my best to cover them in the order they appear.

The *Desire* was an actual slaver that first sailed into Boston Harbor in February 1638; her captain at the time was one William Pierce. My research cannot confirm that the *Desire* ever did sail into New Haven; however, New Haven's slave market was one of the most active in New England and the Connecticut Colony once boasted of having the most slaves of any of its neighbors.

The radio chatter during the attempted search for Jonathan Harris is as true to reality as I could make it. Having been an avid boater on the Chesapeake Bay for nearly twenty years, I was thoroughly familiar with maritime radio traffic and how the Coast Guard coordinated its activities with pleasure and commercial craft alike.

After Jonathan Harris's arrival in New Haven, the Reverend Peter Prudden his traveling companion, Jehu Burr, appear. Both individuals are in my family tree. Burr was Prudden's son-in-law and my ninth great-grandfather, with Prudden being my tenth great-grandfather. Prudden is also believed to have arrived in the American Colonies on board the Hector in 1637 or later. The ocean crossing is fictionalized in Chapter 8 of the first book in the "Lineage Series."

The Reverends Roger Newton and Richard Mather are real. They joined Reverend Peter Prudden on the bench of the ecclesiastical tribunal that tried and convicted Dorcas, sentencing her to a public whipping. The legal system of the Puritan period was entirely based on religion and strict interpretations of the Bible. It should also be noted that Richard Mather was the father of Increase Mather and the grandfather of Cotton Mather – made famous by the Salem Witch Trials of 1692.

The Captain Tettersell that walked Dorcas down the aisle is another real person. In 1651, Tettersell's coastal trading ship, the *Surprise*, spirited Charles II into exile in

France. Charles II later purchased the vessel and renamed it the *Royal Escape*; however, there is no mention of Tettersell continuing as its captain after the royal purchase and renaming. His presence in Connecticut is pure supposition.

Two geographic references in England are also worth highlighting. They are Chillington Hall and Boscobel House, along with the Giffard and Pendrell families. I have anecdotal evidence that I am distantly related to the Giffard line – and the current Lord Chillington. The estate includes Boscobel House and the Royal Oak, both of which factored into Charles II's escape after the Battle of Worcester in 1651.

Posting and reading the banns of marriage predated the modern concept of marriage licenses. The process was mandated by colonial law in 1636 in the English and Dutch colonies. It wasn't until the 19th Century that civil administration began to supplant religion as the regulatory body for marriage. The format presented herein is an approximate representation of the wording that might have been used in the 17th Century.

The Quinnipiac tribe sold its land holdings to white settlers, beginning in 1636 and, thanks to epidemics and forced migrations west, were largely insignificant by the end of the century. The modern Quinnipiac University honors the tribal name and descendants still live in Connecticut. It is not one of the recognized tribes of Connecticut, but the Algonquian Confederacy of the Quinnipiac Tribal Council is dedicated to preserving the history and culture.

Lastly, the intricate circle that is responsible for Bethany's time-hopping is known as "Hecate's Wheel." Hecate was a mythological Greek goddess who rules over the earth, sea, and sky. She was also the goddess of magic and witchcraft, as well as the goddess and protector of entranceways. The wheel is thought to represent rebirth. The "entranceway" and "rebirth" aspects of Hecate's Wheel have no mythological connection to time travel; I took literary license and made the connection to fit the story line.

Acknowledgments

I cannot write a book without acknowledging the support from my darling wife, Sandy. She has always been there for me as the Lineage Series and Lineage Independent Publishing have grown. At times, she does have to remind me that I need to step back into the reality of life; without those reminders, I would get totally lost in the world of books.

Thanks also to my pre-read team and fellow authors, Lisa Talbott, G. B. Carmichael, Rebecca Conaty Bruce, Lorna Hart, and Beck Hilliard. I have used them all as sounding boards as the story "Of Time and Place" unfolded. Their inputs have been valuable in keeping the story on track.

I also have to acknowledge two other people who, though they likely won't admit it, have had huge impacts on the Lineage line. They are Elizabeth Talbott (Lisa's nonagenarian mother), who I can always count on for constructive criticism, and Melissa Speed, who keeps me historically honest. Melissa is also a volunteer "interpreter" (re-enactor) at Boscobel House.

Finally, a huge shout-out to Diane Mezzanotte, a former work colleague and curator of the Oakdale Little Free Library in Laurel, Maryland. Diane's support, especially for launch party interviews, adds another dimension to the Lineage package. She has supported and promoted the books of Lineage Independent Publishing since the company came into existence in 2019.

Other Books by Michael Paul Hurd

Lineage: A Novel

Soldier, Citizen, Settler: Lineage Series, Book Two

Iniquity and Retribution: Lineage Series, Book Three

Wayward Son: Lineage Series, Book Four

The Seventh Wife: Lineage Series, Book Five

The Germans: Lineage Series, Book Six

Uncertain Alliances: Lineage Series, Book Seven

Ground Faults: A Lineage Series Novel

Lineage Independent Publishing
Marriottsville, MD

https://lineage-indypub.com